Agatha
ODDLY

No case too odd...

D0998176

MYSTERIES of

C334341509

Read all the Agatha Oddly adventures:

THE SECRET KEY

MURDER AT THE MUSEUM

Agatha ODDLY

MURDER AT THE MUSEUM

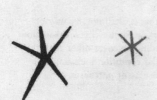

LENA JONES

HarperCollins Children's Books

First published in Great Britain by
HarperCollins *Children's Books* in 2019
HarperCollins *Children's Books* is a division of HarperCollins*Publishers* Ltd,
HarperCollins Publishers
1 London Bridge Street
London SE1 9GF

The HarperCollins website address is
www.harpercollins.co.uk
1

ISBN 978–0–00–821189–9

Tibor Jones asserts the moral right to be identified as the author of the work.
A CIP catalogue record for this title is available from the British Library.

Typeset in 12/20pt Aldus LT Std by Palimpsest Book Production Ltd,
Falkirk, Stirlingshire

Printed and bound in England by CPI Group (UK) Ltd, Croydon, CR0 4YY

MIX
Paper from
responsible sources
FSC
www.fsc.org
FSC™ C007454

This book is produced from independently certified FSC™ paper
to ensure responsible forest management.

For more information visit: www.harpercollins.co.uk/green

For Lizzie and Hannah

1.

RULE BREAKER

'That film was crazy!' says Liam with satisfaction as we step out of the Odeon.

The evening air is pleasantly warm and there are still hordes of people milling around in Leicester Square. We navigate through them. Liam turns his phone back on, while I fish out the last scraps of popcorn from my box. We've just seen the latest crime thriller – *Midnight Delivery* – and can't wait to point out all its plot holes.

'I knew it was the window cleaner,' I say. 'He was far too nosy. And as for the detective – he was *soooo* slow.' I laugh. 'Brianna would've had a field day! Why did she say she couldn't come?' Liam is my best friend, but Brianna is a close second. The three of us hang out together *a lot*.

'Oh . . . I think she had homework,' he says.

I chuckle. 'That figures. One full day left of the holidays and she's finally getting round to it.' Liam and I always get our schoolwork done at the start of the holidays, but Brianna likes to leave it until the last possible minute. I once saw her writing in an exercise book while she was walking down the street to school.

Liam's too busy looking at something on his phone to reply, so I wander over to a bin and dump my empty popcorn box. On a pavement board close by is a poster, with the words *LORD MAYOR'S FIREWORKS!* in big letters at the top. I scan the details. The extravaganza – with 'over 15,000 fireworks!' – will take place beside the Thames, on Sunday.

'Isn't September a bit early for the Lord Mayor's fireworks?' I say as Liam comes over. 'Don't they usually do them in November – around Guy Fawkes Night?' I think some more. 'And I'm sure they're usually on a Saturday.'

He doesn't answer my question, but says, 'Check this out,' and he holds out his phone, so I can see the screen. It's a news alert:

BREAKING NEWS: Murder at British Museum

I stare at the red letters for a moment, feeling a familiar excitement. It's been five weeks since I solved the case of the red slime that had polluted London's water supply, and I'm itching to get going again. Things have been too quiet with no cases to solve, so I haven't been enjoying my summer holidays as much as usual.

I take his phone and click on the link. There's not much information to go on yet:

A member of staff has been stabbed to death shortly after closing time this evening at the British Museum. Police have yet to release the name of the staff member, who is believed to be an attendant who may have disturbed an intruder. A museum exhibit is said to be missing from a display case.

I feel a surge of happiness. 'Finally, an actual case!' I catch Liam's eye as I hand back his phone. 'Come on – we need to investigate!'

He scrutinises me. 'Agatha, tell me you're not actually *pleased* that someone's been murdered . . .?'

My cheeks turn red; hopefully he won't have noticed. 'Of course not.' I study my nails: currently black with silver stars. I'm especially pleased with the stars, which have come out just right.

'Anyway,' he continues, 'it's a murder investigation – you won't be able to just wander in there.'

This is the type of challenge I live for. 'Of course I will. "No Case Too Odd", remember?' I say, reciting the Oddlow Agency's motto. I'd got sick of people making fun of my surname, Oddlow (Oddly . . . Oddball . . . Oddbod . . . Odd Socks . . .) so I'd decided to put a positive spin on it.

'But this doesn't even seem especially odd . . .' he says doubtfully.

Not wanting to waste time, I grab him by the arm and start to stride through the Leicester Square crowds, in the direction of the Tube. Liam stumbles after me, reading the report on his phone.

'It says they've put the museum on lockdown, so nobody can get in there – not even you.'

'Ah, but who said I was going to use the front door?' I look back at him, raising an eyebrow. With my free hand, I touch the place below my neck where my mum's black metal key is hanging from a silver chain. It's not just a trinket: it belongs to a secret organisation called the Gatekeepers' Guild, and it gives access to underground passageways all over London.

Liam frowns. 'You'll be in serious trouble if Professor D'Oliveira finds you using the tunnels before your Trial begins.' The professor is my contact at the Guild. If I want to become an agent, or Gatekeeper, like my mum (and I really, really do), I have to pass three tests that make up the Guild Trial.

I sigh. 'I know . . . but I didn't expect it to take this long to get started! I've been waiting five weeks already!'

'Come on, you know how gutted you'll be if they

catch you – and the professor says you can't take the tests and become a Gatekeeper if you break the rules.'

I roll my eyes. 'But they're not going to notice if I use the key just this one time, though, are they? I'm sure I can dodge them.'

Liam shakes free of my grip.

'Aren't you coming?' I ask, in surprise. Liam normally jumps at the chance of some excitement.

'Agatha, you're my best friend – but you're talking about interfering with a crime scene *and* risking your chances of becoming an agent.'

I decide to focus on his first objection, so I ignore the second. 'I'm not going to interfere,' I say indignantly. 'I'm just going to look for clues . . .'

'. . . And potentially get in the way of the police, who are themselves looking for clues.'

I pause for a moment, wondering whether to try and win him round. But he's wearing his determined look.

'OK,' I say. 'Don't worry about it – you can go and find out what they're saying about the murder on the news. We can compare notes when I see you on Thursday in school.'

'Right . . . just – be careful, though.'

'Oh, it's OK – I'll just dig a tunnel using a spoon,' I say, referring to one of our favourite films.

'So long as you have a plan,' he says with evident sarcasm (spoilt by the fact he's obviously trying not to laugh when he says it).

'I always have a plan,' I reply.

'If there's any more info on the news, do you want me to leave you a note?' he asks.

'Oh, I forgot to tell you – Dad found the loose brick in the wall, so we can't use it for messages any more. He's cemented it in!'

'Seriously? Couldn't you have stopped him?'

I shrug. 'He'd "fixed" it before I got the chance. We'll just have to find a new way of sharing information.'

Liam shakes his head sadly. 'I loved our brick,' he says, as if we've lost a dear friend.

I shrug again. 'Look, I've got to be off, OK? I'll see you at school on Thursday,' and I give him a quick wave then jog the short distance to the Tube station.

On the platform, with five minutes to wait for the train, I feel the adrenaline start to mount. Tonight I'm no longer Agatha Oddlow, scholarship student at a school for privileged kids, but Agatha Oddly, private investigator, named after the world-famous crime writer Agatha Christie.

As the train carries me along, I settle into the rhythm and plan my entrance into the museum. I have a useful ability to 'Change Channel' – switch off from whatever's going on so I can access other parts of my brain. I close my eyes and use this technique now, to focus on the task ahead. I'll be needing a costume and a convincing reason for being at the museum after hours.

By the time I get back to Hyde Park I've worked it all out, and I can't wait to get started.

As I hurry along the path beside the Serpentine

lake I automatically glance at the benches to see if my old friend JP is there, but then I remember JP's no longer homeless, so he doesn't live in the park any more. He's managed to get himself a job, and it even comes with a flat he can rent cheaply. I'm really pleased for him, but I miss our daily chats.

As Groundskeeper's Cottage comes into view, I force myself to focus on my plan. The first thing I need to do is be seen by my dad, Rufus, so that he thinks I'm going to bed for the night. Also, the popcorn already seems like a long time ago, so I should probably make myself a sandwich before I set out.

'Hey, Dad!'

'Hi, Aggie. How was the film?'

'*So* terrible that it was brilliant – really funny!' I go over to where Dad is sitting at the kitchen table, studying some landscape designs for the park, and give him a peck on the cheek.

'That's good. Have you eaten?'

'Only some popcorn,' I admit. (Dad hates it when I skip meals.)

'You should make yourself a sandwich,' he says.

I grin. 'You read my mind!'

I set to work, spreading first butter, then peanut butter, then a layer of salad cream. It's a combination I haven't tried before, but I'm always keen to experiment. I did over-experiment at one point last term, when I attempted to create a masterpiece from a French cookery book. It was disastrous – and I lost some of my confidence – but I'm over that now, and open to new culinary experiences again.

As I stick the two pieces of bread together, I start to go over the details of the plan in my head. I'll need some keys from Dad's collection – he has them to open gates and gratings all over Hyde Park. But Dad derails my train of thought—

'I won't be around tomorrow morning, by the way.'

'Oh? How come?' I look around for the bread knife. Sandwiches always taste better when you cut them into triangles.

'Yeah, I . . . um, I have a meeting with an orchid specialist from the Royal Horticultural Society.'

Something about Dad's tone makes me turn round and look at him.

'An orchid specialist?'

'Yes . . . a very prestigious one . . . and she's only free first thing. So I won't be around when you get up.'

He clears his throat and goes back to studying the plans in front of him, in a too-concentrated way that seems a bit forced. But I don't have any time to worry about what Dad may be up to – I have to get going if I want to inspect the crime scene before the police remove all the evidence.

'OK, I'm going up.'

Dad glances at the clock. 'It's only eight thirty. Bit early for you, isn't it?'

'It's a well-known fact that teenagers need more rest than adults.'

'That's my line,' he says, frowning. 'What are you up to?'

I put on my most innocent expression. 'Nothing. I've just got some reading to do for English, and I want to look over the essays I did at the start of the holidays.' I scoop up my plate and make for the door. 'Don't stay up too late, Dad. See you in the morning!'

'OK . . . night, love.'

I stop on the first-floor landing and creep into Dad's room, where Oliver the cat is curled up on the bed. Dad has a rule about not letting cats on beds, but that never deters Oliver. Slipping the set of keys I need from a hook on his crowded key rack, I place them in my pocket, then start up the next flight of stairs, wolfing down my sandwich on the way. It tastes foul and I make a mental note not to try this particular combination again. I set the empty plate down on my bedside table and look around with satisfaction at my room. It's in the sloping attic space at the top of our cottage and is packed with interesting objects and artefacts, including shells, feathers and fossils, newspaper clippings and elaborate disguises. There's a porcelain bust of Queen Victoria that I found in a skip, plus a chart of eye colours with codes for each shade, which I've memorised. A portrait of my favourite crime writer, Agatha Christie, hangs in pride of place above the bed, and there's a smaller portrait of her most famous character, Hercule Poirot, on the back of the door.

For a moment, my thoughts turn back to the Guild – and, more importantly, the Trial. I've been thinking about it all summer, like a song I can't get out of my head. It makes me nervous, knowing that the first challenge could begin at any moment, even in the middle of the night, and I have to be ready for it. I guess that's the whole point – if you can't be ready at any moment, to act without warning, then you can't be a member of the Guild. But I do wish they'd get it over with.

I take off my red beret – my best-loved item of clothing – and place it carefully in its box. Then I go over to my two rails, where I keep all my clothes and costumes, and start to rummage for the items I need.

Luckily for me, I've already made some notes in my head on the British Museum from my previous visits there. I close my eyes and Change Channel to reach the area where the relevant information is stored. It looks like a series of old-fashioned filing cabinets. I access the one for uniforms and flip through the handwritten cards inside, until I reach M, for 'Museum' – then I select subcategory B, for 'British'. All the British Museum uniforms I've observed have been filed away here, each as an imaginary photograph. I want to get in as an attendant – it's the most convincing role for someone of my age – and the uniform I call up is a simple one: black trousers with a white shirt.

Flicking through the garments hanging from my clothes rail, I pick out a suitable shirt and some trousers. From a box underneath I take a black faux-leather belt and a pair of Doc Martens boots with thick rubber soles that give me a few extra centimetres. They were a brilliant find in a charity shop and I love them. I get changed quickly, removing my knee-length red gingham shirt dress (one of my favourites, also from a charity shop) before pulling on the trousers and shirt. Accessories come next – a work pass on an extendable lanyard which I attach to my belt, and a very basic work badge to pin to my chest, which claims that my name is 'Felicity'. This is the name I use on social media – after detective Hercule

Poirot's secretary, Felicity Lemon. Finally, I tie my hair back in a bun, and for extra camouflage add a pair of thick-rimmed glasses (which are stored in a chest of drawers full of similar accessories — false eyelashes, sunglasses, headscarves, fake scars, bushy eyebrows . . .). I slip the keys into my pocket, along with a small notebook and pen, an LED head torch, a lock-picking kit, and a plastic vial containing a clean cotton bud — an essential part of any detective's kit. My pocket is now bulging, but I don't want to complicate things by taking a bag with me that I might have to abandon somewhere.

Everything done, I look myself over in the mirror.

Pretty convincing.

I don a long plastic mac over my outfit to keep it clean. This monstrosity — the sort of shapeless cover-up sold to tourists who arrive in Britain unprepared for the rain — is not an item I would ever normally wear in public. But needs must.

'See you later, Mum,' I tell the photo of my mother that I keep by my bed. She's wearing a long, flowing skirt, big sunglasses and a floppy hat. I like her style —

comfortable but chic. She's standing astride her bike, which is piled high with books, as usual. The police said it was the books that made her bike difficult to steer – and that was why she'd lost control in an accident with a car and died. But I don't believe that. For a start, I found her bike, and it didn't have a scratch on it. If I can join the Gatekeepers' Guild, maybe I can find out what she was investigating when she died, and it might give me some answers.

Deep breath now – here comes the difficult bit.

I turn my bedroom lights off. If Dad comes up to see what I'm doing, I don't want him to think I'm awake. Then, making my way across the cluttered room by memory, I climb on to my bed. The evening sky is overcast, but there's just enough light for me to make out the rectangle of my skylight. I open this now, grab on to the edge, and haul myself up and out, so that I'm sitting on the roof, straddling the ridge.

I wait for a moment. I like it up here – there's a gentle breeze stirring and, now that summer's coming to a close, the night is neither too warm nor too cold.

Off in the distance, at the edge of the park, I can see the twinkling lights of Kensington. I divide the mission up into phases in my mind: stage one – get away from the house undetected by Dad; stage two – crawl through a long, uncomfortable passage; and stage three – gain entry to the museum. I take a deep breath.

Right: it's time to go.

I ease myself off the ridge and slide down the tiles to the edge, where I cautiously stick my right foot out into space until it makes contact with the nearest branch of the ancient oak tree. The left foot joins it. Next comes the scariest moment, when I push off from the roof and have to trust the rest of my body will get across safely . . . It does, of course – I've been climbing up and down this tree since I was ten. With my arms round the trunk, I feel for my next foothold and make my way down to the ground. I'm glad I thought to wear the raincoat, or my clean white shirt would be covered in moss and lichen by now.

I jump down on to Dad's immaculately maintained

lawn, keeping the oak tree between me and the kitchen window. Dad mustn't see me. Then, taking a deep breath, I run through our gate and off across the park, into the night.

Stage one – complete.

2.

WORK PLACEMENT

To reach the underground passageways governed by the Gatekeepers' Guild, first I have to open a grating beside the Serpentine. I step down the short ramp that leads to the dark, caged-off hole and, when I reach the grating, I fish out Dad's keys and select the correct one. I insert it into the lock – but for some reason I can't get it to fit neatly and turn. I struggle with it for a while before giving up and sitting down on the dewy ground. What now?

I hear Hercule Poirot's voice in my head, with its familiar Belgian accent: '*Venez*, Mademoiselle

Oddlow, we won't let *un petit* lock stop us at the first 'urdle, *n'est-ce pas?'

Poirot may be a fictional detective, but he's my inspiration. Why won't the key turn? Maybe something's stuck in the mechanism. I get up and inspect the padlock. Sure enough, there's a pine needle jammed inside. I form pincers with my thumb and forefinger and manage to remove the tiny obstruction. Then I try the key again. This time it turns, and I swing the grating open and crawl through, pulling it shut behind me.

I shiver, remembering the last time I was down in this dank passageway. The tunnel had been full of toxic red algae, so Liam and I had worn face coverings to filter out the fumes. Even without the stinking slime, it isn't exactly welcoming.

I take the head torch from my pocket, turn it on and slide the harness over my head. The bright bulb illuminates a dirty concrete path. There's a crumbling brick roof that's far too low for comfort, even for a thirteen-year-old of average height, and I have to crouch. I sigh and begin my uncomfortable passage through the long tunnel. It stretches downwards, taking me ever deeper beneath the ground.

Despite the vast amount of earth above my head, I divert my thoughts away from images of the ceiling caving in. My palms and knuckles keep scraping on the stone and brick, and my neck aches badly from having to keep my head bent at an awkward angle. My progress is further hampered because I have to stop every so often to rub my aching leg muscles, which aren't used to staying bent for so long.

I don't realise I'm holding my breath until the corridor opens out into a wide cavern, and I find I'm gasping – dragging in oxygen as if I've been under water. I laugh at myself – I've made the whole journey harder by tensing up and holding my breath! I stretch my back out and give myself a shake. It's such a relief to be able to stand upright.

Stage two – complete.

On the far side of the cavern there's an iron door covered in rivets, like the entrance to an ancient castle. It's so rusty that it's almost the exact shade of the surrounding bricks, making it nearly invisible. Now for the next key: the one I promised Professor D'Oliveira I wouldn't use.

I pull the silver chain out from the collar of my shirt and insert the large metal key into the lock. Mum's key. For a moment, I picture her turning it in secret gates and doors. I feel such a strong link to her when I use it. It turns soundlessly in the well-oiled mechanism. I leave my head torch on the ground, then I push the door open a crack – enough to check for guards, before stepping inside and pulling it closed behind me.

That was way too easy: the Gatekeepers' Guild really should increase their security.

I head down a long, well-lit corridor with a plush, red carpet. After a couple of hundred metres, the carpet gives way to stone as I approach the bike racks. There are hundreds of bicycles here, of all sorts, from high-tech mountain models and off-roaders, to older, more upright models. The Guild own mile upon mile of tunnels, and they prefer to ride through them wherever possible, to save energy and time. For a moment, I try to imagine what type of person owns each model. I spot a large, unwieldy black mountain bike and picture a very severe man in a dark suit. I fix on another one – a pink sparkly, Barbie-doll type – and decide it has probably been borrowed by a parent from their child. I know which one I'm going to use. It belonged to my mum: a baby-blue town bicycle with a basket. The professor promised to keep it here for me.

But it's missing.

I go through the racks, twice, but it's definitely not here. Has someone taken it? Or is it just being stored somewhere safe? I make a mental note to ask the professor about it. I feel a pang at the absence of what feels like a piece of my mum. *It's only a bicycle*, I tell myself. I consider taking another one instead – but that feels more like stealing. I'll just have to jog.

I start to run slowly, building up speed until I'm making good progress along the main tunnel. The ground is fairly smooth here – worn down, I suppose, by years of use by the Gatekeepers. At last I spy a smaller passage off to the right, with a sign for the British Museum. I turn into it and soon reach a full-height metal gate.

Once again, my magic key opens the lock. I step through, close the gate behind me, and abandon my hideous raincoat at the bottom of a short set of stone steps leading up to the museum. At the top, another turn of the key lets me through a wooden door.

I'm in a tiny room that holds nothing but a long staircase, leading upwards, and I jog up them with ease. My fitness levels are pretty good these days as I've been working out a lot over the summer. Before too long I reach what I gauge to be the ground floor. There's a door with a grimy window. I give it a wipe with my hand, and see I'm just off a large corridor. There's no one about, so I slip through the door and easily find my way into the main foyer of the museum.

Stage three – complete.

I know the layout of the British Museum from the many times Dad has brought me here over the years to see the different exhibits, and I walk quietly but confidently through the public section of the building. I meet no one on the way, but I can hear voices as I approach the area where the murder took place. I walk towards the doorway, careful not to draw attention to myself. As I step over the threshold, I take out my notebook and pen and stand poised at the first display cabinet, as if I'm taking notes on the exhibits. If I'm spotted, I'll need to have a good cover story.

Despite my careful planning, I freeze at the sound of a voice quite close, convinced I've been seen. But they're not talking to me.

'So, the piece that's missing is a clay mug?'

I glance over at the speaker. It's a female police officer, with light-brown hair tied back in a ponytail. She's writing in a notebook.

The person she's addressing is a man of about thirty-five, with closely cropped hair and round glasses, which he keeps pushing up his nose. He's clearly anxious – I can see beads of sweat on his forehead. This nervousness, combined with the expensive cut of his suit, suggests he's probably a senior official at the museum. No doubt he'd be feeling distressed that one of the museum attendants, a member of his staff, has died at work. I can't imagine how hard it would be to feel responsible for something like that.

He clears his throat. 'That's right, yes. It's a strange choice for a burglar.'

'How so?'

'Well, you see this piece, right beside the gap?'

I crane my head to get a look but I'm too far away.

'With the lion's head?'

'That's right. Well, that is a very fine example of Etruscan pottery. It's almost priceless. The clay cup . . . well, that's not worth much.'

'So you're saying . . .'

'I'm saying it's odd that a burglar would kill for the clay cup. But perhaps he took the wrong artefact . . .? I still can't believe one of our own museum attendants is dead!'

'I'm so sorry. This must be very upsetting for you. I'll try not to keep you much longer. But the more help you can give us, the sooner we can catch the culprit.'

'I understand—'

'Hey! Where did you come from?' I jump at the voice in my ear and turn to face a male police officer. He frowns. 'You aren't supposed to be here.'

Rookie mistake: I should have kept checking behind me, instead of becoming mesmerised by what was going on in front.

'Oh no,' I say, in an eager voice, 'I am meant to be here, Officer. I'm here on work experience, and I've been in the stores, cataloguing the exoskeletal organisms.' I have no idea if such a collection exists, but I'm hoping to blindside him with long words.

'So what are you doing *here*?' He gestures to the display case. I haven't even taken in the exhibits, but I glance down and see they appear to be fertility statues. I think fast.

'Oh – I finished my work experience tasks for the day and my manager said I could do some of my own work, on my school project – "Fertility rituals of the ancient worlds".'

'Did you not hear the announcement to evacuate?'

I shake my head, wearing my most earnest

expression. 'No, I haven't heard anything. Why . . . has something happened?'

'Surely someone told you this part of the museum is off-limits?' He seems entirely bemused by my presence.

I shake my head again. I need to distract him with a change of topic. Discreetly, I take in as much information as I can, my eyes flicking over his form. There's not much to go on, because he's in uniform, but I do find a few clues.

PET HAIR ON TROUSER LEGS
— dog or cat?

Shoes highly polished —
but with mud on the sides
= a dog that needs walking

Or possibly several, judging by the amount of hair on his trousers

'Do you like dogs?' I say, thinking on my feet. 'I love them!'

His eyes light up. 'I love dogs too! I have four of my own,' he says proudly.

'You're so lucky,' I say. 'I'd love a dog, but my dad won't let me have one.'

His radio crackles and a female voice comes through, issuing instructions. 'Oh, that's for me,' he says. 'Just get your things and go home.'

'OK . . . thanks! I hope my school teacher won't mind too much if I'm late with my project.'

'Can't help you there, I'm afraid. Don't forget your coat,' he says, pointing to a door marked STAFF ONLY. As long as he's watching, I can't head back the way I came in, so I obediently go the way he indicates.

It takes me into another hallway, with another set of stairs leading down. I run down to the basement, wondering if there might be some way back to the tunnel from here. At the bottom there's a door.

I push it open.

3.

CRAWL SPACE

I step inside and quickly shut the door behind me. I'm in darkness and I fumble for a moment before finding the light switch. My nostrils fill with the smell of damp stone.

The single bulb flickers and then comes on; it sheds barely enough light to see by, and casts weird shadows around the room.

The basement itself is ordinary enough – concrete floor and ceiling, with three walls also made of concrete. The fourth wall, facing me, is made of brick and looks older. There are several sets of metal shelves against the walls, stacked with a variety of cleaning products – sponges and mops, buckets and basins, bottles of bleach and disinfectant. There's only one other object in the room, over in the far corner.

It's as big as a bear, and so blackened with age it takes me a minute to work out what it is – a boiler, old and long retired. It was probably left here because it was too much trouble to dismantle it and lug it up the narrow stairs. The squatting lump of metal is knuckled with rivets and valves. There are several water pipes leading up from it, but these have been chopped off, and now stop short of the ceiling.

I sniff the air. Not just damp, but the scent of bleach. This could be from the army of mop buckets down here, but the smell is strong and fresh. By the light of the single, naked light bulb, I look around at the floor, then crouch to run my finger over it. Dust – lots of it.

Over in the corner, by the old boiler, the floor is darker. I walk over. Yes – the concrete here has been scrubbed recently and is still damp. Why would someone clean this patch but not the rest of the room?

In my mind's eye, I conjure up a Polaroid camera. It appears in front of me, hovering in the air. I hold the imaginary camera steady, and start to take some snaps of the room. Each photo scrolls lazily out of a slot on the camera and develops from black to a colour image. When I've taken enough pictures, I file them away in my memory.

Now for my next job. I fish out the plastic vial and use the cotton bud to swab the floor. I could be wrong, but I have a funny feeling about this wet patch. So I place the swab safely back inside the vial for analysis in Brianna's secret lab.

Then I step up to the disused boiler. It's covered in dust and clearly hasn't been used in a very long time. The pipes are cut off, so it can't have leaked. Why would anyone need to clean up here?

Peering into the darkness behind the boiler, I can't make anything out. On my keyring I have a tiny torch, which my dad gave me last Christmas as a stocking filler, so I point it into the darkness. There isn't much there, although . . . I peer more closely. Yes! It looks like there could be a hole in the wall!

I can't see into it from this angle, but the back of the boiler is completely free from dust. It seems as though someone's been crawling around in this area.

There's only one thing for it. Clamping the torch between my teeth, I shuffle forward and crouch down until I'm fully enclosed inside the cramped space. I can see it now, just as I suspected – a hole in the brick wall, big enough for a grown human being to fit through. Looking down at the dirty floor, I can just make out a boot print. Someone has definitely been through here recently!

Steeling myself, I start to crawl forward. My keyring torch doesn't do much to illuminate the space, but by moving the beam around I can see tunnel walls opening up. I wish I hadn't left my powerful head torch in the cavern under the Serpentine.

As I go through the underground passage, the brick surface changes, first to something like concrete, then to a material resembling bedrock, chipped away roughly with a chisel or a small pickaxe. There are no signs of activity here, and it's completely silent. I continue, slightly crouched, but hurrying along.

After about thirty metres, the corridor begins to slope down and, a little further on, the space starts to open out once again. Here, the walls are lined with brick, as the rough-hewn tunnel gives way to a carefully built structure, like a Victorian sewer. Thankfully, this is much cleaner and drier, though!

I carry on, now able to stand up fully, holding the torch in front of me like a miniature shield. Its beam isn't strong enough to fully light the way, and the area ahead looks especially dark and unwelcoming. Until this moment, I've been caught up in the chase. Now, though, I'm suddenly aware of my own smallness. What, or who, might I find down here?

I hesitate. I think of Dad, and my cosy room under the eaves of the cottage.

Then Hercule Poirot speaks to me in the darkness: '*Ma chère Agathe*, you have stumbled upon *un petit mystère*, *non*? You are not going to turn back now?'

Too right I'm not. I push on.

Twenty more steps and the space opens out into

an even wider passage. Here, my tiny light seems brighter than it did in the brick section, because the walls around me are lined with white ceramic tiles which despite being grimy still manage to reflect a little of the beam back towards me. The pale expanse is broken up by bands of tiles in a dark colour, burgundy perhaps, or purple – it's hard to tell in this light under the layers of dirt. But there's something very familiar about them. It takes me a while to realise what it is, out of context as they are.

Of course! These are the tiles used across London to line the walls of Tube stations! In the days when many Londoners couldn't read, the patterns were used to signal the different stations.

Over the last few years, I've travelled through almost all the stations on the Tube map, except for some of the ones further out. I've taken mental pictures of all the tile designs, and I call them to mind now. The pictures appear in front of me as Polaroids, stuck with brass pins to a corkboard that's hanging on the wall.

I check through all of them quickly, but can't

identify the particular arrangement of tiles I'm seeing now – the two burgundy bands separated by a band of white. I turn away from the images.

This is a conundrum – a Tube station which is not a Tube station, right in the heart of London.

I walk a little further, my footsteps echoing back at me. Glancing down, I see dust swirling around my feet. The tunnel is thickly carpeted in a grey lint, which has settled and collected over many years. But I'm not the first person to walk here recently. There are footprints, though how many sets it's difficult to tell because they keep to a track, like when someone walks through snow along the same path that someone else has already trodden down. I think about walking in that track myself, to disguise the fact I've been here, but it's too late – I've already left my prints behind me. A little further down the corridor, I get my first confirmation that this underground building is indeed a Tube station, albeit an unused one – a faded, much-torn poster advertising Ovaltine is pasted to a curved billboard set into the wall.

The poster looks old – very old by the style of

font and the watercolour illustration of a woman holding a steaming mug in front of her. If I had to guess, I'd say it's from the 1930s or '40s, and was put up sometime during the Second World War. But why is it still here? Why was this Tube station abandoned? I walk on, turning this way then that through the empty tiled corridors, and find my answer.

I've stepped out on to a platform. And there, on the wall across from me, is a faded sign, which reads: BRITISH MUSEUM.

It's the disused British Museum station! It's been closed for decades. The people who ran the Tube back then decided that there weren't enough people using it. It wasn't even close to the museum. I know that it used to be a stop on the Central line (that's the line marked red on Tube maps), which for the most part draws a neat line through the middle of London. I wonder whether the Central line trains pass through this station now or just bypass it, going down another nearby tunnel.

As if on cue, I hear a distant, rattling rumble – the familiar sound of a Tube train passing by.

I've always wanted a chance to visit some of the abandoned stations – but I don't have much time to think about that now, because it's getting late and there's a murder to solve – and if Dad has realised I'm away from home, I need to be getting back sooner rather than later.

I search quickly around the platform and find more clues – tiles wiped clean of dust through contact, and, there, a little further along, a dust-free space on the ground, where something was obviously being stored, though it's gone now.

The space is large and roughly rectangular. It doesn't give much of an idea as to what might have been there. When I reach the edge of the platform, I bend down and shine my light into the dark passage. I half expect to see that the old tracks have been ripped up, either to stop trains from passing this way, or so that the metal could be recycled, as happened with many of the city's metal gates and fences during the Second World War. But, as I shine my torch down into the dark canyon, two gleaming bands of silver throw the beam of light back at me. The old rails are not only still in place; they are polished so highly that there can be no mistaking it – trains have passed through here recently, and often.

Hmm . . . how can that be? I've now heard three trains pass by and not one of them has come through. Perhaps they use this tunnel to store trains when they're not in service. Or maybe it's used to store repair vehicles on the tracks. Or could it be a bypass tunnel, which allows trains to pass while another sits idle?

I finish looking around the station, taking mental photos of everything as I go. I wish I had a real camera, so I could get some actual pictures of the boot prints marking the dust around me, but my own memory will have to suffice. I stare at some of them for longer than usual, to make sure that the images are well developed.

Finally, it seems there's no more for me to investigate down here. I could go back up to the British Museum the same way I got down, but the police investigation is well established up there. If I make another appearance, I'm bound to be spotted again, and this time the police might be suspicious. I'm glad I brought my Guild key.

Walking to the far end of the platform, I hop down on to the tracks – and just in time too: I hear the voice of a man, arriving on the platform behind me. Hurriedly, I turn off my torch.

'Did you remember my five sugars?'

I crouch and hold very still.

Another man responds: 'Dunno. I just shovel them in.' So that's two men, at least.

'Jeez, Frankie – you know I can't drink it when it's not sweet enough.'

'I'm just amazed you've got any teeth left.'

They laugh. I can't hear any other voices joining in, but, although it's a relief they're alone, two's more than enough to worry about. I begin to shuffle quickly towards the tunnel, but I lose my balance for a moment and my foot thuds against the metal of the train tracks.

One of the men speaks: 'What's that?'

'What?'

'I heard a noise.'

'Probably one of those mice that live along the rails.'

'Sounded like a pretty big mouse.'

I hear footsteps approaching and flatten myself against the side of the platform as much as possible. Crouching in the shadows, I hope I'm nearly invisible.

A torch is shone along the tracks. It gets worryingly close to me, reflecting in the toe of my boots. I really shouldn't polish my footwear if I'm going to wear it for undercover work. Has he seen me? I hold my breath and close my eyes. I'm clutching my front-door keys, the only potential weapon I have to hand, but I don't fancy my chances if I have to rely on *them* to defend myself.

'Nothing there,' he pronounces, turning and heading back to his mate.

'What time did you say it's due?' asks the other one.

'In the next five or ten, I reckon – if they don't have to stop in a side tunnel on the way.'

While they're talking, I run silently to the tunnel mouth. I know there are several doors on the Central line which will give me access to the Guild passages, and, once I'm in one of those, it will be simple enough to find my way back to Hyde Park. Most importantly, I need to get off the rails before the train comes through.

Inside the total darkness of the tunnel, I dare to turn on my torch again. It doesn't make a lot of difference – the light was dim when I used it earlier in the museum, and it's lost power since then and is frustratingly weak, but it's all I've got. I push on. Five minutes of jogging and I find what I'm looking for – a small wooden door set into the side of the service passage leading off from the Central line.

The sounds of trains on the other tracks are closer now, rumbling and rattling, and screeching as they brake. To some people it could be unsettling – frightening even – knowing that these fast engines are racing through the tunnels surrounding them. But I'm used to this – used to walking underground, used to being a little bit too close to forces that might harm me. Taking the Guild key from round my neck, I don't even pause before putting it into the lock. I'm also growing accustomed to breaking the rules.

Still, after waiting all summer to take the Trial, I can't help but shudder at the thought of the consequences if I get caught down here. I open the door and step into a narrow tunnel which is far cleaner and better kept than the one I've just come from. As I enter, lights come on – automatic sensors picking up my movement. This brightly lit corridor is more disconcerting than the previous one: there's nowhere to hide.

I turn off the little torch and put it in my pocket. One of my brain's tricks is an internal compass that I use to navigate. I have a lot of tools like this – internal filing cabinets and visual memory aids – but I can't explain how most of them work, even to myself. They just do. I walk a little way, passing various doors on my left, until I reach one on my right, which my compass tells me is the right direction for home. I open it and pass through, and walk for fifteen to twenty minutes, checking over my shoulder the whole time. At last, I come to a sign on the wall with arrows pointing in two directions. One of the arrows points towards Piccadilly Circus, the other towards Marble Arch.

Marble Arch is close to home, so I head in that direction. This isn't the most exciting Guild passage, with very little to see in the way of other routes branching off from it, and it's not carpeted and wood-lined like some of the more elaborate ones, such as those that run under Hyde Park. However, it's good to be out of the bright lights of the larger tunnel. It also has a smooth surface, and I begin to jog again, enjoying the rhythmic pace, which lets my brain slow down and start to process the information I've gathered so far.

The maze of underground pathways that runs under London was only partly constructed by the Guild, of course. They patched together several networks, from old Roman and Victorian sewers to modern service pipes, plus parts of the Tube, the electricity board's passageways, the water board's, sections of underground car parks and even telephone exchanges. This patchwork design can be quite useful, because it often gives you a clue as to where you are. In the tunnels I've visited near the South Bank (beside the Thames), the walls are made of an orangey concrete, with two rows of lights down either side. In the tunnels near to Buckingham Palace, they are plush, as though in preparation for a royal visit, and have chandeliers in place of bare light bulbs.

I've never been in this part of the network before, so I make sure I commit it to memory in case I'm ever here again and need to find my bearings. It's weird, heading in the direction of home without any of the familiar landmarks I would have above ground. I'm jogging at a comfortable pace when I hear a faint sound behind me.

I glance over my shoulder.

The tunnel is slightly curved, so I can't see what's making the noise. But I listen very carefully. It's a regular tapping. Perhaps just a leak? No, it doesn't sound like that: it's too regular, and that rhythm . . .

Footsteps.

They're getting louder. Someone's running in my direction. I look back again. As they come round the bend, they're just a shadowy figure. The only thing I can make out is that, when they see me, they speed up.

There's no time to lose. I pick up my own pace, racing like I'm doing the hundred-metre sprint. If the person behind me is from the Guild (and who else would it be, down here in the Guild tunnels?) then I can't let them catch me, or they'll be bound to bar me from taking the Trial. I run and run until my blood is thudding in my ears. My feet are pounding so hard against the concrete that they're starting to throb. At least I seem to be increasing the distance between us, though. After a little while I come to a branch off to the left. I'm dizzy from the run, and have to pause before my vision clears enough to read the next sign. With a sigh of relief, I see it says HYDE PARK ⅓ MILE.

In the brief time I've been standing still, the footsteps have become much louder. The person following me is really close now. With one last push, I race down the offshoot. There's no lighting, but I can make some out ahead, filtering through from the far end of the tunnel. This passage is also straighter than the one I was just in and, after a few moments, I glance back into the darkness and see a torch heading through the darkness towards me.

My forehead is dripping with sweat and my breathing is becoming painful. I keep glancing back, and the light is still there, following a little way behind. Whoever's chasing me can't catch up, but they're not falling back either. Off in the distance I see it at last – a spiral staircase leading up from the tunnel floor.

It takes an almost Herculean effort to make it up the stairs. I have to stop partway up because my calves are aching badly. I bend over, panting and rubbing my legs, convinced my tracker will reach me. Then the area below lights up from their torch, and that's enough of an incentive to send me climbing again, up and up, above the roof of the tunnel.

Finally, the spiral staircase ends. I see a small iron door in front of me; I put my Guild key into the lock; and, just as my pursuer's foot sounds on the bottom rung of the metal staircase, I step through the door, out into the cold night air, and shut the door firmly behind me, panting loudly.

The moon is bright and full, showing me that the door is set into a stone embankment, near the Serpentine lake. I'm not far from home and I don't have time to stand around. After taking a second to get my bearings, I race away across the lawns, into the night.

Usually, when getting home late, I climb back up the oak tree and in through the skylight. But there's no way my legs will cope with that tonight. Plus, it's so late that all the lights are off in the cottage. Dad must be in bed. I don't want to spend any more time outside than I need to, not when somebody might still be tailing me. So I take out my house keys and, as quietly as possible, go in through the front door.

I collapse in the hallway, leaning against the front door and breathing heavily. The excitement of the evening, and the chase through the tunnels, have worn me out. But my mind's as alert as ever, buzzing with ideas and theories, with images from the museum and the underground station.

I decide to get myself a glass of milk. Maybe that will help me get to sleep. There's no point in me staying up all night, trying to solve a case where I don't have all the facts. I will wake up rested tomorrow and start again, with Liam and Brianna to help me.

It's dark in the kitchen, but I don't want to turn the light on. The moon's shining through the window and it's just about enough to see by. I open the fridge, letting out a refreshing blast of cold air. I take out the milk, close the door, and turn towards the cupboard, where the glasses are kept.

As I do, I jump, so startled that I drop the carton of milk on the floor.

There's someone standing in the corner of the kitchen, waiting silently in the shadows.

I stumble away, pressing my back to the work surface. Without taking my eyes off the intruder, I feel for a knife in the knife block. But my silent companion doesn't move. I focus hard on their outline. There's something not quite right about this person.

Walking over, I flick the light on.

For a few seconds, I'm blinded. But then I can see what startled me – one of Dad's old suits. It's hanging on a coat hanger from a hook on the wall, a double-breasted jacket over the trousers below. This is a particularly offensive article from Dad's wardrobe: double-breasted brown twill with mustard pinstripes. Someone should have been arrested for creating this suit. And someone should definitely arrest Dad for wearing it. Knowing him, he'll probably team it with a mustard shirt and his favourite green tie. I love him dearly, but his fashion sense could do with some help.

Dad said he had to visit another gardener in the morning, but why would he be putting on a suit to visit an orchid specialist? Especially a suit he hasn't worn in years – a suit which, though it's hard to believe, he thinks is very flattering. I walk up to the offending outfit and tentatively sniff it, and the smell it gives off confirms my suspicion – this suit has recently been dry-cleaned. It looks smart: pressed and lint-rolled of even the slightest speck of dust. Who is Dad trying to impress?

I pour myself a glass of milk, replace the carton in the fridge, turn out the light, and begin my weary climb to bed. I navigate my way upstairs, avoiding the creaky steps. I'm conscious that I'm still wearing my disguise and am now streaked with grime from the dirty tunnels through which I've been running and crawling. If Dad were to see me now, like this, his suspicions would certainly be raised.

Dad knows I love investigating, but I think he imagines that I'm out looking for people's lost cats, or watching for shoplifters at the corner store. Not that there's anything wrong with either of those, but I have bigger fish to fry. Dad doesn't know about these bigger fish: about the Guild, or about the work they do, protecting the capital from the plots of dangerous, greedy people.

Which is for the best really.

I can hear Dad snoring loudly as I climb the stairs. At the top, a sudden 'Meow!' makes me freeze. Oliver has come to welcome me. He purrs loudly and pushes his stocky body against my legs.

'*Shhh*, Oliver!' I scoop him up with the arm that isn't carrying the milk and let him drape himself round my neck. It's far too warm for this, but I love feeling his vibrating purr. I wait for a moment, to make sure Dad's still snoring, then creep up the flight of wooden steps to my attic bedroom.

I set Oliver down gently on the floor and look around me. Everything is laid out as I left it, but it seems like I've been gone for so much longer than a few hours – as though I left yesterday, or a week ago.

Adventure is a bit like that – you feel as though you've been moving very fast, and the rest of the world has been moving very slowly, and you can't quite believe that it's still Wednesday, or whatever day of the week it is, because it seems like you've lived a week – a month, a year! – in a short space of time. I suppose I like this feeling a bit too much – I rely on the adrenaline rush to keep my life from getting dull – but I try not to worry about that.

I go over to sit on my bed and sip at the glass of

milk. I wonder if Mum ever felt like this, when she was a Gatekeeper. You don't get into this line of work if you don't like excitement – if you don't thrive on risk. Did she worry that one day her escapades would get her into serious danger? Or did she live her life from day to day, not worrying about what tomorrow would bring? I look over at her photo on my bedside table.

Looking at this picture usually makes me feel sad or wistful, similar perhaps to what I'd feel if I was looking at a picture of a house that I used to live in – a happy memory. But, tonight, I don't feel sad or wistful.

I feel angry.

I decide to analyse this new response. I run through what I know – and don't know – surrounding her death:

1. Whatever happened to Mum, it wasn't a bike accident.
2. I have a hunch that her death was linked to her work as a Gatekeeper.

3. *Someone's covered up what actually happened – could it have been the Guild?*

I realise my new anger is because I've just had a close encounter with someone who almost certainly belonged to the organisation. I feel something close to rage at whoever caused Mum's death – but also at whoever hid the truth from Dad and me. I close my eyes and focus on my breathing until I've calmed down enough to turn the rage into determination.

'I will find out what happened to you, Mum,' I promise her photo.

Finally, with no energy left to think or feel, I get under the covers, drink the last of my milk (thinking how Mum would have scolded me for not brushing my teeth) and turn the light out. Just before I drift off, I remember the swab that will need analysing. I grab my mobile, switch it on, and send Brianna a text, asking if I can go over to hers the next morning. Then I let sleep pull me under its thick surface.

4.

THE BLACK BAMBOO

I wake up late and check my mobile. Brianna replied at about 2am.

Sure. Come over whenever

I don't know what she was doing up in the early hours, but I guess I'll find out when I see her.

I pull on my dressing gown and head down to the kitchen. Dad and the brown twill suit have both gone. He's left me a note:

Gone to that meeting I mentioned

May be back late.
Help yourself to croissants.

Croissants are my favourite. I'm just cynical enough to suspect he's done something wrong – or is planning to do it – if he's buying me my favourite breakfast food. This doesn't stop me accepting it, though. I eat a croissant, down a glass of orange juice, then go up for a shower before getting dressed. I choose one of my mum's floral shirt dresses over a pair of jeans. I add a wide black belt to cinch in the dress, and top off the ensemble with a denim jacket. I love wearing Mum's things – it makes me feel closer to her. I toughen up the look with my Doc Martens boots.

I stuff a couple of croissants in my jacket pockets and munch on another as I head across Hyde Park towards Cadogan Place. It's quicker to walk to Brianna's than take public transport. It's close to noon, and the air is muggy for early September, but the light is glorious, gilding the trees.

I turn into Sloane Street, the home of super-expensive designer shops like Louis Vuitton and

Chanel. Brightly coloured flags fly outside the embassies for Denmark, Peru and the Faroes. A black cab driver has got out of his vehicle next to the Danish embassy. He's on his knees, unwinding what looks like a long piece of black plastic bin liner from one of his back wheels. I recognise him as one of the drivers from the taxi rank outside the park.

'Hi, Aleksy!' I call.

'Hi, Agatha. Just look at this mess. I wish people weren't so careless with their rubbish,' he says. 'This could affect my brakes if I don't get it all out.'

'Is there anything I can do to help?'

'No, that's all right, thanks. No point both of us getting filthy.'

'OK, if you're sure. Good luck!'

'Thanks!'

I leave him and continue my walk. I demolish the last croissant at the corner of Brianna's road, and dust the pastry flakes off my hands.

When I reach the grand townhouse on Cadogan Place, Brianna throws open the door. She couldn't look less like a CC these days: there's not a trace of the over-manicured mannequin that Liam and I loved to hate, before we got to know her. The CCs are the Chic Clique, a group of annoying, wealthy, smug girls, all with identical long blonde hair, thick make-up and manicured nails, that go to my school. Brianna's hair – which has been dyed a brilliant sky blue, cut to chin length and then shaved on one side – is sticking up messily at the back, and her black eyeliner is smudged, giving her panda eyes. She looks like she hasn't slept in weeks.

'Fantastic shade of blue!' I say, ruffling her already ruffled hair, and she grins and gives me a hug.

'Thanks! Thought it made a change from last week's pink.' She pulls back to look at me. 'I love the dress. Another one of your mum's?'

I nod, happily, and follow her as she leads the way to the study, where she seems to spend most of her time.

'Have you slept at all?' I ask as I follow her through the massive, marble-paved hallway. 'You look shattered.'

She shakes her head. 'I'm doing research into how long a person can survive on no sleep.'

'Really? How long have you managed so far?'

She squints blearily at her watch. 'Ummm . . . something like thirty hours?' She sounds unsure.

'Isn't sleep deprivation one of the ways they torture people?'

She grins 'Yeah. But it's a bit different when you're safely at home.'

I'm confused. 'So how does this fit with you wanting to be a forensic scientist?'

She shrugs. 'I want to get inside the heads of criminals, so I'm trying out a few torture methods on myself.' She sees the look of alarm on my face and quickly adds, 'Just the easy, painless ones – a dripping tap, sleep deprivation, that kind of thing.'

'Your mum and dad are away again?' I ask.

'Do you need to ask?'

Her parents (or 'seniors', as she calls them) are always travelling to glamorous locations, leaving Brianna in the care of her rather careless and frequently absent older brother.

'Missed you at the cinema,' I say. 'It was a good one.'

'Yeah – Liam said. But I had way too much to do.' She leads me through to the study, where I stop in surprise at the sight of Liam. He's sitting in a chair at the desk, leaning back with his feet up. His face breaks into a beam when I enter, and he gets up and hurries over.

'Hey – great to see you.'

'So, this is why I'm here . . .' I begin.

'You mean it's not just for the pleasure of my company?' says Brianna, pouting.

'Stop doing that with your face,' I tease her. 'You remind me of when you were in the CCs – all fake pouts and baby voices.'

She shudders. 'Don't. I can't bear to remember it. Was I awful?'

'Awfully awful,' I tell her gravely. 'You're lucky you've got me and Liam now to keep you grounded.'

'Did you hear about the horrible thing Sarah's done to me?' she asks. She means Sarah Rathbone – queen of the CCs and her ex-best friend, of course.

'No, what's happened this time?'

'She's posted awful pics of me again, all over Instagram. She's Photoshopped them, so I look like I've got really bad acne.' She hands me her phone, and Liam and I study the pictures. Brianna looks quite different when she's covered in pimples.

After a moment, Liam nods approvingly. 'That's pretty skilled work. It must've taken ages to make the spots look authentic.' Brianna doesn't seem offended.

'Oh – she had help. She's got a cousin who's really good at editing photos.'

I hand back the phone. 'So why is she doing it this time?'

Brianna is trying to look nonchalant, but I can see it's hurt her. 'Just part of her ongoing campaign to humiliate me.' She shrugs. 'For deserting the posse.'

'Nice,' I say, pulling a face.

'At least it confirms I made the right move, leaving the CCs,' she says.

'I heard they were holding auditions for your

replacement,' says Liam. 'Wasn't there some girl who bleached her hair because she was so desperate to get in?'

'Yeah, Cherry-Belle McLaughlin – you know, the footballer's daughter.'

'The one with all that long black hair?'

Brianna pulls a face. 'Not any more. Now it's bright orange and she's having treatment to try and stop it breaking from the bleach damage.'

'Ouch!' I say, and Liam nods in agreement. There's a word, Schadenfreude, which basically means taking pleasure in other people's pain or misery. As the year's 'misfits', 'geeks' or whatever you want to call us (I prefer 'mavericks'), we've been on the receiving end of far too much Schadenfreude to relish other people's misfortune.

'So,' says Liam, pointedly changing the subject, 'how did you get on at the museum?'

'OK.' I pat my pockets. 'I've got a swab sample I'm hoping Brianna will analyse for me.' I produce the vial containing the cotton bud.

'Where did you take it?'

After I fill them in about what happened at the British Museum, Liam makes a low whistling sound of admiration. I feel myself blush.

'So you really did manage to get in then?'

'Yeah.'

'That's our girl,' says Brianna. She yawns and stretches. 'Not sure how much longer I can stay awake, by the way,' she says apologetically. She checks her watch and makes a note in an open exercise book. 'Thirty-one and a half hours,' she murmurs.

'Did you use the Gatekeepers' key to get in?' Liam asks me. I frown a warning at him: we're not supposed to talk about the Guild in front of Brianna. 'You know you're going to get murdered if the professor finds out.'

But Brianna doesn't seem to be listening. She's walked over to a light switch near the bookcases on the back wall of the study. She flicks the switch casing open and presses a keypad. A section of the bookcase swings back. I never tire of seeing this: it's such a classic secret-room device. If I ever envy Brianna, it's not for her huge house, nor for the library (and I do mean an *actual* library, in its own room, with a high-up reading area like a balcony) – but for her secret room filled with all the paraphernalia a detective could ever dream of. She's collected so many gadgets and chemical testing kits in her private lab over the years, as long as she's been dreaming of becoming a forensic scientist. I feel pretty lucky to have got to know her – not just for her gadgets but for our shared love of all things investigative.

But while we've been distracted by the bookcase, Brianna has slumped against the wall, her eyes closed. 'Sorry, but I need to sleep now,' she murmurs. 'Can we do this later?'

'Of course,' I say. I drag one of the curve-back study chairs over to her side and Liam helps me manoeuvre her into it. He finds a blanket in another room and drapes it over her.

Once we're satisfied she's comfortable, we walk inside the secret lab. Liam hasn't been in here before and he stops on the threshold, taking in the extraordinary sight. It's just how I have remembered it. Metal shelving fills the walls, and there are all sorts of tools and equipment on every shelf, including test tubes, pipettes, Petri dishes and bell jars. I walk past Liam, running my hand along a row of bottles containing various substances arranged in alphabetical order from acetic acid to zinc. I take mental pictures of all the supplies – just in case I ever need something.

In the centre of the room there's a stainless-steel table furnished with a Bunsen burner. I'm itching to set the flame alight, but I hold back. It's not mine, and I should really wait for another day when I can ask Brianna whether I can come and try out some experiments.

'This place is amazing!' says Liam.

'I know. I wish I had one.'

'Hey – at least she's willing to share it.'

'True.'

We're silent for a moment, studying the room. Then Liam says quietly – not for the first time, 'Brianna's not at all what I expected.'

'I know. She's not all about her Instagram image at all.'

Reluctantly, I take a final look around the room

of sleuthing treasures. 'OK – better close this up, I guess – I don't feel like I should use the equipment to test the swab without her.'

We come back out and close the bookcase, and I place the vial on the mantelpiece, with a page torn from my notebook propped up behind it, bearing the words *Please test me!*

'OK,' says Liam, 'shall I walk you to the Tube?'

I laugh. 'It's broad daylight, in a built-up area – I'm pretty sure I don't need an escort. But we can walk together if you like.'

We head out of Brianna's house, making sure the front door latches properly behind us. The street is quiet as we walk towards the Underground station, and the air has become even more muggy, as if Liam has draped a blanket over not just Brianna, but the whole of London too. When we get to the Tube, he gives me a quick wave.

'See you tomorrow,' he says.

My heart sinks. School! How will I ever do the Trial when I'm stuck in a classroom all day?

I watch him walk off to his bus stop. I know his

walk so well, I could pick him out in any crowd: swift and eager, as if there's always something good round the next corner.

I don't go home. I'm due at my martial arts lesson with Mr Zhang. I'm not sure why I haven't told Liam about these lessons. After all, he knows pretty much everything about my life. If I'm honest with myself, it's probably just that I want to be much more proficient before I share it with him. At the moment, I'm little more than a beginner. Vanity affects us all to some degree, I guess.

This is a new pursuit for me, which was suggested by Professor D'Oliveira. Actually, 'suggested' is too gentle a verb. Her exact words were: 'If you're going to be running about London like a headstrong fool, you'll need some decent skills.' I'd bridled at that. I had plenty of skills, many of which she still knew nothing about.

Still, she'd given me Mr Zhang's card and said to tell him Dorothy had sent me.

The martial arts gym (called a *dojo*) is beneath Mr Zhang's restaurant – the Black Bamboo – in the Soho area of central London, which he runs with the help of his granddaughter, Bai.

I open the wooden door and step inside. Bai is sitting on a stool at the bar, surrounded by textbooks. She fits working at the restaurant around her law studies. Bai stands politely to greet me. She is tall and slender – she always reminds me of a silver birch tree; her hair is long, and today she's wearing it knotted at the nape of her neck. She's dressed in a silky sheath dress with an all-over print of poppies.

'Hi, Bai. You look lovely.'

She smiles. 'Hi, Agatha. Thank you. I love your dress! You can change into your *gi* in the back room.'

Bai gestures for me to go through a curtain made from vertical strips of coloured plastic. It leads to a tiny room at the back, where I quickly remove my dress and jeans and don my white *gi*, which I've brought in my backpack. I fold my clothes and place them on a chair, with my boots underneath. I stop for a second to study a symbol framed on the wall above the chair.

I know it's the symbol for biang biang noodles. Mr Zhang has explained that it is one of the hardest symbols to write in the Chinese language. The story goes that the symbol was invented by a poor scholar who didn't have any money to pay for his bowl of biang, so he offered the cook a symbol to advertise his dish. It's so complicated that there's still no way to type it on computers or phones. Luckily, there's a mnemonic for writing it by hand. Mr Zhang taught it to me:

Roof rising up to the sky,
Over two bends by Yellow River's side.
Character eight's opening wide,
Speech enters inside.
You twist, I twist too,
You grow, I grow with you,
Inside, a horse king will rule.

Heart down below,

Moon by the side,

Leave a hook for fried dough to hang low,

On our carriage to Xianyang we'll ride.

I leave the room and descend a set of red-tiled stairs to the basement. *Back underground, where I belong*, I think to myself, with a wry smile. I seem to be spending all my life in basements and tunnels at the moment.

Mr Zhang is waiting for me when I open the door. He is dressed in a black suit – his *gi* – and his grey hair is scraped back from his face and fixed in place with what look like chopsticks. Mr Zhang frequently loses personal items such as his glasses, his house keys, or the special sticks he uses to hold his hair in place. One time when I came, he was hunting for a pen, and I had to point out that he had two in his hair. For a true master of his trade, Mr Zhang can be surprisingly flaky.

We bow to one another and I approach him, barefoot, across the wooden floor. I would love to say that Mr Zhang lunges at me and I defend myself with a skilful move, throwing him halfway across the room – but my lessons aren't like that. Instead, he instructs me to work through the 'forms' he's taught me so far – the sequences of movements which will, eventually, lead to more complex skills.

When I finish, there is a long silence.

'You have been practising these forms?'

'Yes.' I have been doing them every morning and evening throughout the holidays. I only forgot last night and this morning, with all the excitement of the new case.

'Hmmm.'

I stand and wait for his judgement.

At last, he clears his throat and says, 'We will take some tea.'

He leads me to a little table, at which we each take a seat, and he pours jasmine tea from a decorative pot into small matching cups without handles, like tiny bowls. All of the china at the Black Bamboo features the same pattern: a delicate, sketch-like outline of bamboo canes and leaves on a white background.

I love the way the tiny cup feels in my hand – smooth, warm and fragile, like a soon-to-hatch egg.

We don't talk for a while. I'm trying to learn patience, but it defeats me eventually. 'Was I that bad?' I ask my *sifu* (my 'master teacher').

'Bad? What?'

'My forms . . . were they so bad?'

He nods. 'Ah, the forms.' He leans his head to one side in a pensive pose. Then he pats my hand gently. 'Do you know the expression "The one who waits wins"?' Mr Zhang has countless similar expressions, each of which he presents as if it's a wise adage, handed down through hundreds of generations. Between you and me, I suspect he invents them himself.

I shake my head.

'Ah. You must learn the art of patience, dear Agatha. Only then will you achieve true balance and expertise.'

I wait, but no further wisdom comes. Instead he says, 'Chocolate biscuit?' and holds out a plate of Penguins. 'I like the jokes,' he confides.

We finish our tea and biscuits and then I do some

training with a broadsword. This is my favourite part. Not all beginners get to practise with serious weapons like the broadsword – but apparently Professor D'Oliveira insisted I be fast-tracked to gain competence in the wielding and safe use of basic weapons.

'Good, good,' he says, his head on one side. 'Now adjust your stance, just so . . .'

After my class, I head back up the stairs to the antechamber where my clothes are waiting. But something is different: on top of my folded floral dress is a tiny white parcel. I pick it up.

As I look more closely, I realise that it's not a parcel but a flower; a perfectly folded piece of paper in the shape of a bud. But what is this unlikely bloom doing here, on my clothes? Did Bai put it here? It's so complex that I can't imagine how each fold was created to achieve this elaborate design. As I peer closely, I think I can make out some writing inside – but I don't want to risk damaging the paper by attempting to open it along the wrong folds.

I decide to ask Bai about it. Cradling the paper creation gently in my palm, I walk through the strip curtain to the restaurant. Bai is perched on a bar stool, making notes from a textbook. She looks up as I approach.

'What have you got there?' Her face brightens as she sees the origami. 'Oh! It's lovely!'

'You didn't make it then?'

She looks astonished. 'Me? I don't know how to do origami.'

'Let me take a look.' We both turn to see Mr Zhang. He is adept at moving silently, and we haven't noticed him arriving upstairs. I hold out the flower for his inspection.

'This is very advanced origami,' he says.

I nod. 'Who do you think left it here?'

'You found this here?' He thinks for a moment, and I think I see a slight twitch of understanding move the features of his usually inscrutable face. 'Does it have any words on it?'

'Only on the inside, where I can't get at them.' I stare at the bud again and spot a tiny inked symbol on one of the petals. 'There is something here, though – is it a Chinese character?'

Bai takes the flower from me and says, 'It's the character for water'.

'Fetch her a bowl of water then,' says her grandfather, in an uncharacteristically impatient tone. I decide that now wouldn't be a good time to quote his own saying about patience back at him.

Bai fills a china bowl at the bar sink and places it on the counter. Mr Zhang nods at me to float the bud on it, but I hesitate. What if all the ink runs, and I can never read the hidden message? But my mentor is waiting, so I take a deep breath and gently set the closed flower on the surface of the water.

We all watch. For a moment, nothing happens. Then, a single petal opens slowly. There is another pause, and then the next petal begins to unfurl, followed by another, until they have all opened and the tight bud has transformed into a beautiful flower. There is classical music playing in the restaurant and it feels as if the bloom's unfurling is part of the symphony. It reminds me of those documentaries that use time-lapse photography, missing out whole chunks of time, so that a shoot emerges from the earth and a flower blooms, all in the blink of an eye.

On a flat plane at the centre of the flower there are some words, in tiny writing, as if a fairy has dipped a wren's feather in ink. Above the message, there is an outline: the key symbol of the Gatekeepers' Guild. My hands are shaking now. It has to be the start of the Trial! This must be the first of the three tests . . . and I'm not . . . I'm not prepared. *Call yourself a detective, Agatha Oddlow?* I think to myself.

We all lean over the bowl and I read aloud:

'"Come visit me, in these Dutch gardens."'

Beneath this, still in the tiny writing, is a stream of . . . gobbledygook, which I don't even attempt to read aloud:

CHOO-CHOO RIBBIT PLOP OINK JANGLE PLOP CHEEP KERPLUNK
VROOM WHIZZ OINK WHIZZ BELCH CHOO-CHOO JANGLE OINK
JANGLE BRRING BELCH THWACK CHOO-CHOO HONK HONK BELCH
JANGLE MOO GUFFAW CHOO-CHOO RIBBIT PLOP OINK JANGLE
BELCH THWACK PLOP JANGLE MOO CHOO-CHOO PLOP HONK
WHIZZ ACHOO JANGLE BUZZ BELCH BELCH THWACK PLOP BANG
THWACK GUFFAW WHIZZ OINK BEEP BANG THWACK PLOP MOO
PLOP BRRING JANGLE MOO PLOP JANGLE BRRING CHOO-CHOO

BELCH CHOO-CHOO BELCH HONK DING BUZZ HONK BELCH WHIZZ
BELCH THWACK CHOO-CHOO OINK QUACK — BELCH THWACK
WHIZZ BELCH THWACK WHIZZ KERPLUNK KERPLUNK PLOP OINK
PLOP BEEP

'What is that?' asks Bai. I shrug, but I can feel excitement kicking in. It's a coded message. At last, an opportunity to put my code-cracking skills to the test!

'A cipher?' asks Mr Zhang, and I nod. 'Let's bring the girl some more tea and leave her to work.'

I set myself up at the bar, on a high stool, with my pencil case set before me and my notebook open at the next blank page. The restaurant isn't due to open for another couple of hours and Mr Zhang and his granddaughter leave me in peace to work. I Change Channel and access the part of my brain that shuts out the world, allowing me to focus on the task at hand. I believe it's the same state as in hypnotherapy – a semi-trance.

I scan the message. The code is a basic cipher. I underline each word that repeats frequently – these probably represent vowels or common letters, such as T or S. Then I underline pairs of the same word, which could be L, P or T, as these letters frequently double up in words (*yellow, letter, swallow, matter, pepper* . . .).

I'm soon working it out . . . *WHIZZ* = A and *PLOP* = E. One by one, the other letters fall into place, and the words begin to reveal themselves to me – *the, I've, of.* I've decoded A, T, H, E, O, F, N, D, S and W. The rest of the letters now swiftly offer up their identity – it's like a game of hangman, filling in the blanks.

The finished message reads as follows:

I've no explanation of this story. I've no theories about the why and wherefore of it. It's just a thing – that happened.

I recognise it at once as the opening sentence of Agatha Christie's 'In a Glass Darkly', a short story from a collection of Miss Marple's final cases. Mum used to read it to me when I was little. I've always had a taste older than my age when it comes to books. But what's the connection now? I look back at the first part of the riddle – 'Come visit me, in these Dutch gardens.' Why does that ring a bell . . .? Of course! I've seen an English Heritage blue plaque dedicated to Agatha Christie on the house where she lived, at 58 Sheffield Terrace – in Holland Park!

I go in search of Bai and Mr Zhang and find them bent over a game of cards at one of the restaurant tables. Bai looks at me shyly.

'I should really be helping in the kitchen,' she says, 'but I have a bet going with Grandfather.'

'What kind of bet?' I ask.

'That he will lend me his car on Saturday night, if I beat him.'

'Go for it!' I tell her.

Mr Zhang looks up from the game. 'She will not beat me,' he says, calmly. He studies me for a moment. 'You are going?'

'Yes. Thank you for everything.'

'You got . . . what you needed?'

'I did.'

He smiles and winks (honestly, *winks* – he never ceases to surprise me) and I head out of the restaurant.

I have to catch the Central line from Oxford Circus to Notting Hill Gate. There's then a nine-minute walk to Sheffield Terrace, according to Google Maps. I make it in seven and a half.

Number 58 is a grand, white, four-storey townhouse with a set of steps up to the entrance. I feel a thrill of excitement at the thought that Agatha Christie lived here. I can't resist standing on the pavement and closing my eyes to Change Channel. I can see two maids coming down a back staircase, carrying bedpans and dirty linen. Agatha is sitting in a back room, overlooking the gardens. She's at the Remington portable typewriter that she used to work on, composing the crime that will befall her next unwitting victim.

I come back to the present and focus on the test I've been set. All the buildings on this side of the street are fronted by a tall wall, and the blue plaque is high up on the house, beside a first-floor window, which means I can't get a good enough view from the pavement.

However, the door in the wall from the street is

open and there's a smartly dressed man on the doorstep of the house (dark suit and tie, white shirt, neat hair, polished shoes – a doorman?).

I call out, 'Please can I come closer?'

When he smiles and nods, I walk through the archway and get as close as I can to the blue disc – but I can't see anything from the foot of the house that I couldn't make out from the pavement. There's nothing extraordinary about the blue plaque; nothing that appears newly added or freshly painted.

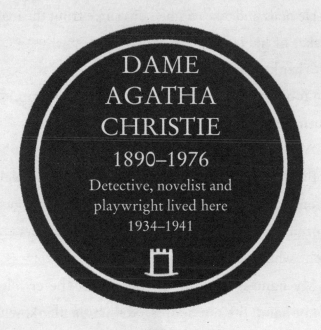

DAME
AGATHA
CHRISTIE
1890–1976
Detective, novelist and
playwright lived here
1934–1941

I'm so engrossed in looking at it that I forget all about the man I thought was the doorman. I jump when he says, 'Are you looking for something in particular?'

I smile. 'Sorry – I'm just a big fan . . .'

'Miss Oddlow?' he enquires, and I stare.

'Er, yes . . .'

'Do you have a title for me?' he asks.

I frown, until I understand. '"In a Glass Darkly",' I reply.

He nods and takes a small envelope from the inside pocket of his jacket.

'Thank you,' I say.

'Your mother was a wonderful woman,' he murmurs.

'You knew my mum?'

But he just nods to me once again – in farewell – before striding down the steps and away. So, not a doorman but . . . an agent for the Gatekeepers. An agent who knew my mum.

My hand is shaking as I glance at the envelope in my hand. It's not addressed – just a blank, white rectangle of thick, high-quality paper. I'm dying to open it, but this is far too public a place. With regret, I slip it inside my backpack and head home, reflecting on the encounter. That man had known my mum. I wish I'd run after him, instead of just standing there, clutching the envelope he'd given me.

The minute I step inside Groundskeeper's Cottage, I take the envelope from my backpack and tear it open. Inside I find a single, small square of paper, bearing simply the letter A. I reflect on the possibilities – A is for . . . so many things! Agatha, of course – Christie and Oddlow. Then there's 'agent' and 'accident' and 'alibi' . . .

There's little point in attempting to solve this clue until I have more information. I'm sure it's one part of a message that will become clear with the next two tests of my Trial. I've finished the first test – I've cracked the code, I've got the letter A, and I'm on target. I'm on my way to becoming a fully fledged Gatekeeper!

I wander through to the kitchen, where Dad is in his dressing gown and cooking chips and fish fingers – I can tell by the smell.

'How come you're in your pyjamas?' I ask, going over to kiss his cheek.

'Hi, Aggie. Oh, I didn't want to get anything on my best suit.'

'Actually, a bit of decoration might improve it . . .'

'Ouch! Are you being rude about my clothes again?'

'Dad, if you would only let me take you shopping—'

'But I like my wardrobe!'

'I'd just like to see you in something more flattering.' Dad is powerfully built – tall and broad-shouldered – so he should wear clothes that complement this. 'Anyway, give me a chance. All I want is to dress you more tastefully . . . and a little less like someone from an old gangster movie.'

'A gangster movie? Really?' He looks worried.

'Are you wearing aftershave?' I ask him. It's a rhetorical question. He reeks of the stuff.

'Maybe a little.'

'A little? You've piled it on so thick it's practically becoming an organism in its own right. Any minute now it's going to grow legs and walk out of here.'

He pulls a face at me. I notice, though, that he doesn't offer any explanation for his sudden interest in smelling good (or his version of it). I'm still elated at solving the first part of the Guild Trial and I'm willing to let it go – after all, Dad has his secrets, and I have mine.

But when we sit down together to eat dinner, I see how distracted he is. Watching him push his food around the plate and forget to put it in his mouth, I can't help wondering whether he's found a girlfriend. Is he about to replace Mum? The thought creates an actual stab of pain in my chest.

'Are you all right, love?'

'Yeah, just a bit of heartburn.' I lie. At the end of the day, who am I to deny my own father happiness?

'So . . . back to school tomorrow,' he says.

'Yep.'

'Are you looking forward to seeing your friends?'

I pull a face. 'My friends are mainly just Liam and Brianna – and I've been seeing them all summer anyway.'

'Be good to put those "leetle grey cells" back to use,' he says, doing a bad impression of Inspector Poirot's Belgian accent. I groan and he laughs. 'Come on – you go and rest – I'll clear up here.'

'Thanks, Dad.'

I give him a kiss on the cheek then go up to my room, where I take out my school uniform, laying the blazer over the back of my bedside chair, with the skirt, shirt and tie on top. Rummaging through my underwear, I find a pair of navy tights and add them to the pile. Then I line up my school shoes underneath. The clothes are so drab that I feel my heart sink. Time to customise the outfit . . .

I flick through the scarves that are knotted along one of my two clothes rails and select a square one with a vibrant print of birds and flowers – it's by the designer Mary Quant, from the 1960s. It's not regulation uniform, so I won't get away with wearing it for long in school, but at least I can brighten up my walk over there.

For the rest of the evening, I indulge myself by re-reading a collection of Hercule Poirot stories, while musing on the significance of the letter A. I fall asleep, running through the possibilities in my mind. *A is for apple; A is for aardvark; A is for algebra. A is for . . . Alabama. A is for abracadabra; A is for . . . aconitum . . . A is for . . . arsenic . . .*

5.

THE SINKHOLE

I wake up far too early. The sun is streaming through my skylight. *First day back*. At least there are only two days to get through before the weekend. They're breaking us in gently.

I leave in good time, my scarf neatly knotted round my neck. As I walk to school, through the park and along pavements not yet crowded with tourists, I mull over that letter A from the first test. After a while, I return to my original theory that it must be the first letter in a word. Hopefully, the second test will point me in a specific direction.

When I arrive at St Regis, ready to start the new

school year, the playground is already buzzing. There's a whiff of excitement in the air; it's not only a new term, but we're also skiing down the slope towards the season of presents. There are a lot of different religions at the school – kids come from all over the world to enjoy its 'rarefied atmosphere', to quote the prospectus ('rarefied atmosphere', aka snobbery and elitism), but they all seem to exchange gifts at Christmastime. It's a great unifier.

Anyway, here we are, at the start of the school year. Students stand in clumps, catching up on gossip. Students who haven't seen each other for a few weeks are keen to catch up, wanting to share what's happened to them and find out what their friends have been up to. Of course, most of them have posted their entire six weeks in stylish Instagram pictures – posing with handsome family members on yachts or outside luxurious holiday homes. Around half the students have been home to Africa, India, Malaysia or China. The rest have been swanning around with the 'It' crowd in French or Swiss resorts, or lazing on Caribbean islands. It's only those students like Liam and Brianna, whose parents seem to have forgotten they have kids, or me, whose dad can't afford a luxury holiday, who have simply been hanging out together in London for the best part of the whole holiday.

Of course, the excitement of the new school year will have fizzled out by about two thirty, with the realisation that a whole new term of work is ahead of us. They'll have told all the jokes they'd saved up, and there will be double physics to get through before home time.

But, for now, the new term is crisp and fresh. Like everyone else, I cast my eyes around the playground for my group. My friend-set is not as big as some, perhaps. There are groups that have ten or more key people in them, plus others who come and go. In a far corner of the playground, I spot Liam and Brianna, standing together. Liam spots me, says something to Brianna, and they both look towards me, smiling as I approach.

'Agatha!' Brianna shoots me a grin.

'Hiya,' I say, smiling back. 'You look better: did you get a lot of sleep after we left?'

'I slept like a baby.' She beams.

'But do babies actually sleep well?' says Liam doubtfully. 'My aunt has a baby, and he screams all night. She's permanently exhausted. Oh . . . here.' He hands me my morning paper, which he always pinches after his guardian has finished with it each morning.

'Thanks,' I say, and I scan the headlines. Nothing of immediate interest, but I'll read it properly later, to check.

'How are you?' Liam asks. He looks at me searchingly.

He's talking about the Guild Trial, of course, but doesn't want to say so in front of Brianna.

I smile, and nod, to let him know it's started, at last. He grins back, understanding how important this is to me.

Brianna glances around to see if anyone is close enough to overhear. Then she leans towards me. 'I analysed that swab you left for me . . .' she says.

'Great! And . . .?'

'Well, I could be wrong . . . I mean, I'm not a professional . . .'

I can feel a tingle of excitement. I know what Brianna is about to say.

'Yes, but . . .?'

'OK . . . I think there were blood traces in that swab.'

I take a deep breath. My suspicions have been confirmed – the murder probably took place in that basement. As only the corner near the old boiler and the opening was bleached clean, it's likely that the tunnel is an important part of the puzzle. Had the attendant stumbled on something he shouldn't have seen? Had he been done away with for knowing too much? I shiver for a moment, realising he might have crawled through the same entrance as I had – and only a short time before me, wanting to find out what the crawl-hole was doing there. I'd been fortunate enough to get away with my investigating, but he hadn't.

'You OK?' Brianna asks.

'Yeah . . .' I'm about to thank her for her work when a shrill voice interrupts me—

'Hey there, supergeeks!'

It's Sarah Rathbone. I haven't seen her for several weeks (unless you count her Instagram updates), but – apart from a tan – she hasn't changed much. She still has the same sheen of blonde hair (how come she never has a strand out of place?), the same manicured nails, the same subtle but expensive jewellery. But then why would she change, when she's already put so much effort into perfecting *this* look? Of course, it used to be Brianna's style as well; she used to be perfectly primped and preened, with her own curtain of blonde hair.

I haven't forgotten some of the things Brianna said and did to me when she was Sarah Rathbone's friend, nor all the things she did to other people too, but I have forgiven her. People can change. And, in the case of Brianna, with her half-shaved, all-blue hairstyle and her battered leather jacket from Camden Market (and goodness knows what Dr Hargrave, our headmaster, is going to say about those), the change is very evident—

'Get lost, Sarah.' Brianna beats me to it, meeting the gaze of her former friend with a steely glare.

'Ouch! That hurts,' Sarah drawls, rubbing her cheek as if she's been slapped – but a grin is spreading across her face. She knows she's hit a nerve.

'I just wanted to say hello to you *both*,' Sarah says, putting a strange emphasis on the last word. She's looking from Liam to Brianna, and I guess she's just making a point of how insignificant she considers me. She was furious last term, when I became something of a celebrity for solving the problem with London's water. She turns to me, seemingly as an afterthought.

'Oh, hi, Agatha. *Oddly* enough, I didn't see *you* there.' I manage not to react to this well-worn misuse of my surname. 'Well, catch you all in class.'

And with those words, and a snigger, she disappears.

I sigh. 'Nothing like the Sarah Rathbone welcome back, is there?' I say.

'Tell me about it,' says Brianna, and she dashes off after a boy she knows from maths. 'Hey! Adedayo! Wait up – I want to ask you about that project Foghorn set us. She didn't actually expect us to *do* it, did she?'

Liam remains quiet for a moment, watching Brianna go. Then he says, 'So, come on, tell me about the –' he glances around him and lowers his voice – 'first test. Have you done it already?'

I smile, my mind taken off Sarah Rathbone's behaviour for the moment, and start to tell the story of the Guild's test, the curious riddle and my trip to Holland Park. (I leave out the fact that I started at the Black Bamboo, and am rather vague on the location of the origami flower.)

I relish Liam's reaction, which somehow makes the experience more real. After waiting for the Guild Trial for so long, it seems amazing that it's finally happening. Or, at least, it has begun. If it weren't for recounting the tale, and seeing the look on his face, I might almost think that I'd dreamed it up in a fever pitch of expectation.

'A letter A?' says Liam. 'Is that all?' He sounds disappointed.

I nod. 'Yeah. But it's only the first test, remember? I'm guessing the other two will help provide the answer.'

I'm so engrossed in our conversation that I completely forget to look in detail at the newspaper – until right before the bell goes to call us into school. When I do, I see a small article at the bottom of page two, under the headline:

SINKHOLE SWALLOWS ICE-CREAM VAN IN BERNIE SPAIN GARDENS

I read the article, my interest piqued. The Bernie Spain Gardens are on the South Bank, next to the River Thames and close to the Tate Modern art gallery. The idea of a sinkhole opening up in such a prominent location sparks something in my thoughts, though I'm not sure what.

This is what being a detective is like, to some extent – you just get a tingling feeling at the back of your head, and you have to trust that your instinct is leading you somewhere – somewhere productive, somewhere you might discover a clue. But of course, the more you listen to the tingle, the more often it might lead you astray. Too many times I've ended up hiding behind a tree, or disguised as a barista in a coffee shop I don't work in, just because I trusted the tingle and set out on a wild goose chase.

But then, if you never followed it, if you never trusted your instinct, you'd never have any adventures. So should I trust it now, or should I ignore it and go to my first class of the day?

As we walk towards the front door of the school, I turn to Liam and ask, 'What's our first lesson?'

'Double maths, of course,' he replies, practically rubbing his hands together with glee. Liam enjoys maths; I don't. For him, it's as enjoyable as a blockbuster. For me, it's about as enjoyable as . . . well, about as enjoyable as double maths first thing on a Thursday.

'Oh, right . . .' I reply, somewhat distractedly.

Liam must see something in my expression, a glint in my eye. 'Oh, Agatha, no,' he says.

'What? What is it?' Brianna asks, joining us at the entrance. She looks between us, trying to decide what's going on.

'Nothing,' I say.

'She's planning to skip school,' Liam replies.

Brianna turns to me. 'Really?'

I was going to tell a white lie, but, under the intensity of her gaze, I realise I can't. 'Er, yeah . . . There's something in the paper I want to check out.'

Unlike Liam, Brianna smiles, as though giving me her approval. Liam's been putting up with me running off on investigations for some time, whereas to Brianna it's all quite new, and she's still amused by what she sees as my rebellious streak. She doesn't realise it's not rebellion – it's just me doing the work I was born to do. And school is just something which, rather unfortunately, gets in the way of my investigations.

'Well then, I think you should go.' She pretends to study my face with concern. 'You're looking quite peaky. That stomach ache must be bad. Come on, I'll show you to the gates.'

And Brianna escorts me across the playground, one hand on the small of my back, as though guiding someone who might have a fainting fit at any moment. Grateful for her acting, I play along, bowing my head and crossing my arms over my stomach. Nobody tries to stop us, though I'm aware of several people looking in our direction.

The groundskeeper, Mr Perkins, is standing sentinel at the gates when we reach them. 'Where are you two going?' he growls.

'I'm not going anywhere,' Brianna replies, 'but Agatha here is feeling very unwell, and she's already put in a call to her dad, who's coming to meet her.'

Mr Perkins opens his mouth, obviously about to raise some objection to this, but Brianna speaks first, lowering her voice as if confiding in him: 'She's got woman's problems. You know how it is.'

Mr Perkins clamps his mouth shut, clearly embarrassed by the idea that I have a female body – or, indeed, any body at all. He nods me on. Brianna pats me gently on the back and says, 'Get well soon!', and I'm on my way down the road.

I know that Liam and Brianna will do their best to cover for me in form class and beyond, and Liam still has his clever box which has a recording of me saying, 'Here'. It probably won't get me through the day, but it might get me as far as lunchtime, and that's probably all I need to investigate the sinkhole and sneak back in for lunch.

Getting to the South Bank is easy enough from St Regis. I take a bus most of the way and hop off at Westminster Bridge. I walk along the South Bank for ten minutes, until I come to the Oxo Tower, which marks the start of Bernie Spain Gardens. Looking out across the lawns, which are all too rare in this crowded part of London, I can see a circle of yellow-and-black tape fluttering in the breeze, a dark hole in the lawns, and – with its tail end upended like the *Titanic* mid-sinking – an ice-cream van with its sign partly obscured. I recognise the logo, and I know the name – 'Mr Cool Cones' – as it's often parked outside the school gates at home time.

I start to walk towards the circle, taking note of everything around me as I go. There's a white van with a satellite dish on the roof parked quite near to the sinkhole, and some people milling about outside it: clearly a news crew, come to get footage.

Sinkholes are more common in areas like London that have clay soil, because it swells when wet and shrinks when dry – most sinkholes are caused by earth shrinkage. It doesn't help that the clay is Swiss-cheesed with tunnels, and sometimes one of these will collapse, and take the surface world down with it like a yawning mouth.

There are a few tourists and locals who have stopped to look at this spectacle, as though it were another art installation on the South Bank. Really, the sinkhole isn't all that big, though certainly big enough to swallow the ice-cream van, which still has its back door thrown wide open, presumably from where the ice-cream vendor made his escape.

From the description in the paper, I had expected the hole to be huge, like ones I'd read about that had swallowed whole streets, but it's around the size of a double-decker bus. It's made to seem much bigger by the circle of yellow-and-black tape, which, because the authorities are not sure whether the sinkhole might extend and widen, has been placed cautiously far from the perimeter of the hole itself.

I go up to the tape, wondering if anyone will stop me if I duck underneath and walk closer to get a better look. I can't see what is at the bottom of the hole – can't see whether, for instance, there's some sort of cavern underneath, or whether the hole is just a sagging indent in the earth, as though a giant hand from above has pressed its finger into the soft grass. My own fingers are on the tape, and I'm about to lift it, when a voice speaks, very gently, from right beside me.

'You need to forget this. Stop investigating.'

I spin to face the person talking, and see a woman wearing a hoodie, with a scarf pulled over her face and dark glasses. It's an effective disguise. She's unidentifiable – even her voice is muffled.

'Why? Who are you?' I say, startled.

The woman says again, more urgently, 'You need to stop this, Agatha Oddlow. Stop investigating.' And, without another word, she walks away from me, towards the South Bank, and disappears into the crowds.

I could run after her, of course – ask how she knows my name, ask how she knows I'm investigating. But something stops me and holds me back. Perhaps it's her manner, plus the fact that she walked up to me here in broad daylight and spoke my name as though she were an acquaintance of mine, an old friend. That takes a certain degree of confidence and I know confidence is often a sign of power. People who can afford to protect themselves tend to have little to fear.

So I let her go. Only Liam knows I was heading for Bernie Spain Gardens, and if I vanished from here, in the company of this heavily disguised woman, the trail could easily turn cold. If something happened to me, no one would know where to look. My mind goes back to a little more than six weeks earlier, just round the corner from the Royal Geographical Society, where someone had reached out from the shadows, clamped a chloroform-soaked rag to my mouth, and whispered in my ear to stop investigating.

This is what they always want, of course, the corrupt people I find myself up against – to stop my investigations. They always pretend it's a choice I can make; they're just giving me some 'friendly advice', they're only telling me 'for my own good'.

Well, they can keep their advice.

I walk round the sinkhole for another minute or two, taking in details, but also keeping an eye out for anyone who might be watching me. The news crew begin their broadcast beside the hole, and I make sure to stay out of shot.

Finally, I'm done, and I stroll away from Bernie Spain Gardens, right down the South Bank, in the direction of the Tate Modern and, further along, Shakespeare's Globe, the reconstructed Elizabethan theatre. The weather is still mild and a little humid, so I take off my blazer and put it in my backpack.

I lean against a railing for a moment, looking out over the Thames as it crawls past, on its way to the sea. Seagulls bob on its surface, and a tourist boat passes, filled with people holding cameras. I take out my mobile phone, switch it on, and send a message to Liam, asking him to research the geology of Bernie Spain Gardens, and anything underneath which might have caused the cave-in. When it's sent, I switch the phone back off and continue on my way.

I often find that walking helps me to think. It's the same as staring out of a train window – something about the movement lets your brain relax, and all the problems which seemed so hard before suddenly make sense. The *little grey cells*, as Poirot would say, start to work.

Written notes appear, tattooed on to the foreheads of the passing tourists . . .

Warned off . . . Who? Why?
    Is sinkhole above a Guild tunnel?
        Is it connected to museum murder?

The link with this last question seems tenuous at first. But the more I consider it, the more likely it seems. After all, the person who warned me must have been watching me for some time – otherwise, why would they follow me to the sinkhole? And if they've been watching me, they know I'm investigating the British Museum case.

And, together, these two facts add up to create a third: quite simply, I'm on to something big. For the first time in six weeks, this is a real case.

Content that I've done everything I can for the time being, I buy myself a hot chocolate from one of the stalls that line the South Bank. Then I make my way back towards Westminster Bridge, ready to get the bus to St Regis – and the necessary evil that is geography class.

Getting back into school isn't quite as easy as getting out of it, and involves hiding from a PE teacher, crawling beneath a chain-link fence and scrambling through a shrubbery.

Luckily, Liam and Brianna have done an admirable job of convincing our form and maths teachers that I'd been sick enough to need to return home. In fact, I have trouble convincing my geography teacher that I'm over my stomach ache and sickness now, and am well enough to be in school.

I sit through geography, listening to facts I already know about tectonic plates and continental drift. After that, it's time for lunch in the canteen, which St Regis calls the 'refectory', to keep the snobby parents happy. It's there that I fill in Liam and Brianna about what has happened on the South Bank.

Liam is especially concerned, and keeps saying, 'Agatha, please don't take any more risks. You'd better stop investigating.'

Brianna's response is: 'She must be on to something if they're warning her off.'

I smile at her gratefully, but Liam just looks more worried. 'Exactly! She's on to something, which means whoever murdered the museum attendant could be coming after her!'

'I hadn't thought about her life being in danger like that,' says Brianna.

I sigh. 'Will you stop talking about me in the third person? I'm sitting right here – and quite capable of making my own decisions.'

'Are you, though?' says Liam. 'I mean, look what just happened to you.'

I poke at a lump in my custard with my spoon. 'I'm fine, aren't I? Stop making such a fuss.' I glance at him. His eyes are wide with anxiety, so I say, reassuringly, 'I'll be careful.'

'Promise?'

'I promise.'

In the afternoon, we have history (which I enjoy), computer programming (which Liam enjoys) and ballroom dancing (which nobody on earth enjoys).

By the end of the day, I'm dog tired. I drag my weary body through the front door, and hear Dad in the kitchen – he's home early. I go to greet him.

'Hey, Dad.'

He's making himself a cup of tea. 'Hello, love!' he says, with a big smile. Something about his behaviour is still unsettling me – he's too *perky*.

It's a long time till bed, but Dad has once again already changed into his dressing gown and pyjamas, together with the fleecy slippers I gave him last Christmas. The dreadful double-breasted brown suit has obviously made another appearance – it's now draped over the back of one of the kitchen chairs. I can see a red line round the back of Dad's neck, where the itchy wool has rubbed his skin. Even he can't bear to wear the thing for too long.

'Do you want a hot drink?' he asks. 'You look tired.'

I laugh. 'Oh, cheers – now I feel really great.'

'You know what I mean.' Dad smiles, comes over and envelops me in a bear hug. He really is in a good mood. I break out of it and look up at his face, quizzically. I can't read his expression.

'Yeah, I'll have a hot chocolate, if that's OK.'

'I'll put the milk on. I've got us a couple of pizzas for tea.'

I sit down at the table and study him as he sets to work. He's humming to himself.

'Dad?' He turns and meets my eye with his head on one side. 'How come you've finished work so early again? And why do you keep wearing your suit?'

'Oh . . . I took a couple of days' leave. And I had that meeting with the orchid specialist, remember?'

'Yeah, you told me about that – but since when

did gardeners wear suits to visit other horticulturalists? And I thought that meeting was yesterday.'

He looks uncomfortable and busies himself, placing the pan of milk on the hob to warm and then setting the oven temperature for the pizzas. When he straightens up, his shoulders are squared, as if he's steeling himself to tell me something bad. He's twirling a tea towel between his fingers.

'Aggie, we need to talk about something.'

He sits down opposite me. Here comes bad news – I'm sure of it. My chest feels constricted, like I'm wearing a corset that's been pulled way too tight.

Dad clears his throat. He's still twisting the tea towel between his fingers. 'It was a very important horticulturalist . . . and the meeting went so well that I had a second one today.'

'This meeting . . .' I say. 'Was it a date?'

Dad looks startled. 'No! What? Agatha, why would you think that?' He seems genuinely shocked, as though the possibility of him going on a date hasn't even occurred to him. 'Date? No, I had a job interview.'

There is silence in the kitchen, except for a sizzle

as the milk rises to the rim of the pan. Dad leaps up just in time to rescue it, then pours it into a mug for me and spoons in the chocolate powder.

I'm confused. 'Why are you applying for jobs? I thought you loved it here.'

He sets the mug down in front of me. 'I do, but I didn't apply – they headhunted me.'

'Who did?'

Dad takes a deep breath, and I have a sinking feeling in my stomach. I don't know what's going on, but this doesn't feel good.

'It was an interview with one of the managers from the Eden Project.' He pauses, and lets this sink in. 'It went so well yesterday they followed up with a second interview today. And they came to London specially to see me.' He can't disguise his excitement.

'But . . isn't the Eden Project in Cornwall?'

'Yes . . but, look – I haven't even been offered the job yet,' Dad protests, looking guilty. 'They said they'd get back to me in the next day or two.'

For a moment, my head is too full of thoughts for me to respond. If Dad takes the job, it would mean moving away from my friends, away from the Guild . . . Cornwall might be lovely, with its sandy beaches and palm trees, but leaving London would mean an end to my life as I know it.

There are a thousand reasons why I don't want to leave the capital, but one keeps coming back to me.

London is Mum's city.

This is where she was born, where she lived, where she died, and now where she's buried. I have to stay here, to be close to her.

'I just – I wish you'd told me this was going on,' I say, rather lamely.

Dad looks sheepish. 'I was always going to tell you. I thought the interview would go terribly, anyway. I was only going to go out of curiosity.'

'So the second interview went well?'

'I didn't say that! They were nice . . . Oh, I don't know.' He runs his hands through his hair until it stands up all over. 'This could be a fantastic opportunity for me. What do you want me to say?' His voice is almost pleading.

'That you have no intention of taking the job. That

we're not moving to Cornwall. That I'm not going to have to leave my friends behind.' Tears are streaming down my face and my voice is coming in gulps. I push back my chair and stand up. 'I – I'm going up to my room. I'll come and get my pizza when it's ready.'

I retreat upstairs, feeling bewildered and powerless. I can't open up and tell Dad about the Guild, and all that it might mean for my life – and for finding out how Mum died. My mind is churning, and I just lie on the bed, staring up through the skylight, unable to stop thinking about it all.

After a while – I have no idea how long – there's a soft knock on my door.

'Aggie?'

'Come in.'

Dad pushes open the door. 'I've brought your hot chocolate up – it was going cold.'

'Thanks.' I sit up and he hands me the mug.

'Pizza'll be done in a few minutes,' he says. He stands awkwardly for a moment, then picks up the clothes from the chair by my bed, looks around for somewhere to put them, gives up and piles them on the floor. He sits down.

'Look, Aggie – I didn't mean to spring this on you . . .'

'Will you take it? The job?'

'I don't know. It would be a big step up in my career. They want to train me up as senior management.'

'Wow, that's great.' I smile, but it's weak. 'Dad . . . on the day, you know, when Mum . . .' I leave it unspoken; it's still hard to say the word *died* – 'I was just wondering what they told you – what the police told you, I mean.'

Dad shakes his head sadly. 'What's brought this on again, love?'

I hesitate. 'It's just – if we're going to be moving away from Mum . . .'

He nods. 'I understand. But I've told you everything I know, Aggie – what the police said to me; what the paramedics said to me; what the witnesses said to me . . .'

I sigh, knowing this is true – Dad's remembered

and recounted everything he knows. But, somehow, I can't help going back to it. All I want is to gain access to the Guild files on Mum's death, because I know there's something going on, and I know someone is keeping information from me. Once I've become an agent, I should be granted access to the file rooms, including any files there might be on Mum – including the case she was working on when she died. Waiting to get access to those files is driving me crazy. Once the Trial is over—

'I just worry, love, that you're going over things too much.' Dad breaks my train of thought. 'It's not healthy. It won't bring her back.'

'That's not what I'm trying to do.'

He pats me on the knee. 'Just try to let it go.' He stands up. 'I'll see to those pizzas.'

'Dad, I'm sorry for how I reacted about your job.'

'That's all right, love. I don't blame you – it's quite a bolt from the blue, isn't it?'

I nod. 'So do you think they'll offer it to you?'

'I really don't know. Let's wait and see, before we start to panic, shall we?'

I smile and nod. 'Are you going to watch your gardening show?'

'Or we could eat together up here instead, if you like?'

I shake my head. 'No, that's fine. Just my pizza, please.'

He salutes smartly. 'Aye, aye, ma'am!'

I stick my tongue out at him and he laughs. Five minutes later, I'm sitting on my bed, tucking into a margherita pizza with black olives, and Dad's downstairs, watching TV.

I glance over at Mum's photo. 'Isn't it funny how food can make you feel better?' I ask her. She smiles and I toast her with my empty mug.

Several hours later, I pad softly downstairs to the kitchen to make myself another mug of hot chocolate. (Whatever people say, I don't think you can have too much of a good thing.) Dad's sitting in the living room, with the telly still on, and he doesn't hear me opening the fridge for the milk. I'm quite glad to be alone with my thoughts. I decide that I'll make a list of positives about moving to Cornwall, just in case. So far, the list only has two points:

1. More sunshine
2. Less pollution

I've heard there's an island off Cornwall where cars aren't even allowed, only bicycles. Perhaps we could live there – it would be like living in a different time period, which I've always dreamed about.

I finish making my drink, wash up the pan and creep back upstairs. I place the mug on my bedside table and lie back down on my bed while I wait for the cocoa to cool. That's when I spot it: a square of white on the other side of my skylight that I'm sure wasn't there before. It looks like an envelope . . . It shines as brightly in the moonlight as if it had a spotlight trained on it. For a moment, I can neither move nor take my eyes from it. Finally, I find the willpower to act. I stand on the bed, open the skylight, and haul myself out just far enough to grasp the paper. I drop back inside and close the window.

I sit on the end of my bed and turn the envelope over, slowly and cautiously, as though it's a venomous creature that might bite. I smell it to check for traces of poison, but it just smells of bleach and ink. It's a fine-quality envelope, made from densely woven fibres. The name on the envelope – and it's only a name, no address – is neither mine nor Dad's, but that of Felicity Lemon.

Could this be the second test in the Trial? I'll just have to put my Cornwall list on hold for now.

I clear a space on my cluttered desk, pushing aside a plastic replica of a human skull (filled with pencils), several vinyl LPs from Camden Market, a Perspex box containing the dissected contents of an owl pellet, and a thick Victorian tome on the subject of blood-spatter patterns.

At last, I rip the envelope open. Inside is a single piece of paper, with a list of nine email addresses typed on it in black ink. *Helvetica font*, I note. A bit old-fashioned, but nothing special.

1. Samantha Octavius – soctavius@twofatladies.net

2. Matt Parlance – matty@talktoomuch.au

3. Samantha Helix – samh@andshout.com

4. Alan Gardener – agardener@flourish.org

5. Majid Mustang – maj@hihosilver.org

6. Janice Corona – janco@overhead.com

7. Alice Selena – ally@crescent.com

8. Stanislav Hasp – stan@captainjames.net

9. Emmeline Jaunt – emmybean@fairground.co.uk

I scan the list several times, and realise this is a fairly simple cipher, at least to begin with. There's something in the name and something in its corresponding email address that together point to a word. In the case of Stanislav Hasp, for example, the surname is another word for a hook; and the Captain James in his email address could refer to Captain James Cook, the explorer, or maybe Captain James T. Kirk, but I'm sure that it refers to Captain James Hook, from *Peter Pan*. So both the name and the email address are pointing me in the direction of one word – 'hook'.

The other eight are the same.

By the end, I've listed nine words. The last one to give me trouble is Samantha Octavius, until I remember that Octavius is from the Latin word 'octo', which means 'eight', and 'two fat ladies' refers to the bingo call for the number 'eighty-eight', so the answer is simply 'eight'.

So now I have my list of words – eight, speech, twist, grow, horse, heart, moon, hook, ride.

Here is where things get difficult. Finding the words was a little tricky in places, but really no more difficult than doing the cryptic crossword in a Saturday newspaper. Figuring out what the sequence of words means, however, is totally different. I stare at my notebook. Have I seen these words before? There's something at the back of my head, something that I can't quite grasp. This is what it's like sometimes with solving clues. It's as though another part of my brain has the answer, but doesn't want to give it up.

I close my eyes and Change Channel, picturing the words on a blackboard above my head. Then the words go fuzzy and I hear someone speaking them. The voice is Mr Zhang's. My eyes flick open.

I've come across this sequence of words before, and not that long ago. They're from the mnemonic poem for drawing the symbol for biang biang noodles! I run through the poem in my head.

Roof rising up to the sky,
Over two bends by Yellow River's side.
Character <u>eight</u>'s opening wide,
<u>Speech</u> enters inside.
You <u>twist</u>, I <u>twist</u> too,
You <u>grow</u>, I <u>grow</u> with you,
Inside, a <u>horse</u> king will rule.
<u>Heart</u> down below,
<u>Moon</u> by the side,
Leave a <u>hook</u> for fried dough to hang low,
On our carriage to Xianyang we'll <u>ride</u>.

Biang biang noodles are an unusual dish, and there aren't many places that make them. Luckily (though perhaps not surprisingly), the Black Bamboo claims to serve the best biang in this hemisphere. It was there that I first saw the complicated Chinese symbol – so where else could the riddle be wanting me to go?

It's late, but there will still be people in the streets. If someone is following me, I'd rather not stand out. Quickly I change into a neat black sweater and black leggings. I tuck my chin-length hair into a black cap. I'll probably be a bit warm, but at least I'll look nondescript.

A quick check in the mirror, and then I make for the skylight. The night is cooler than I expected, and a slight breeze whips around me. I'd forgotten how tired I was until now, balancing on the roof, making for the tree. My body aches from my run through the tunnels the night before last, but it moves on autopilot as I start to climb down the branches. I'm so full of adrenaline that I can't think of anything but the riddle, and getting to Soho as quickly as possible.

I reach the ground and, silently, with my back to the house, start to run across the lawns, out into the darkness of Hyde Park. I settle into a jog and keep up a steady pace, out of the park gates and on into the night.

The streets are quiet and London has an almost deserted feeling as I push on through Soho and finally come within sight of the Black Bamboo. There are no lights on in the shops and cafés on either side of the restaurant, but through the misty glass of the restaurant I can see a lamp is still lit. I hurry over to the door, taking in everything in the window: the red and gold decorations, the pictures of cats happily waving, and there, in the cards showing the various dishes, the symbol for biang.

I hesitate before knocking on the door, running over the riddle in my head, in case I've missed anything. I'm sure this is where I was meant to come, but what if I was supposed to bring something with me? Or knock on the door a certain number of times? I can't think of anything, but, just to be certain, I knock on the door nine times, like the nine clues in the riddle.

After a brief wait, I see a shadow moving in the

gloom behind the glass, then the unmistakable form of Mr Zhang unlocking the door, sliding bolts and removing chains. The door opens inward and he's standing there, silhouetted in the light, a small smile playing on his lips. I'm a little out of breath, but Mr Zhang is perfectly still. He's clearly happy that I'm here, but his head is tilted, as if he wants to hear something specific from me. There is only one thing that I can think to ask:

'I'd like a bowl of biang biang noodles . . . do you have any?'

The small smile breaks into a full grin, and Mr Zhang seems to breathe a sigh of relief. When he remembers himself, he nods seriously, steps back from the doorway and ushers me into the empty restaurant. The chairs are up on the tables, and there's the smell of floor cleaner in the air. Perched on a stool behind the counter is Bai, in her dressing gown, and yawning widely.

'You made it!' she calls. I wave and she waves back.

Wordlessly, Mr Zhang points to a table, so I go over and sit down, while he disappears behind the counter and into the kitchen. Now that I'm further into the restaurant, I can smell, not just floor cleaner, but something else – a rich, brothy smell. Something is already simmering away, ready for me.

I listen to the sounds of Mr Zhang working in the kitchen, though these are sparse. There's no clattering of pots and pans when you're a trained martial arts master: everything is graceful and controlled. Bai just sits on her stool and grins at me. Her gaze makes me fidgety. Is she waiting for me to do something?

'Should I . . .?' I begin to ask aloud, but Bai just grins more widely for a moment and puts a finger to her lips. She shakes her head.

No talking then. OK.

I sit in the darkened restaurant, stomach rumbling a little at the delicious smells that are snaking out of the kitchen, but my mind is fully focused on the test. I'm so restless, waiting to discover the next part, waiting to find out if I pass, that I'm practically squirming in my chair.

After what seems like at least half an hour, but is only ten minutes according to the clock above the counter, Mr Zhang reappears, with my food balanced on a tray. Bai follows him over to my table, and the two of them take seats opposite me. The bowl of steaming noodles is pushed towards me, and I inhale a lungful of fragrant steam.

Biang biang noodles are strange things, which is why they have become known as one of the eight strange wonders of Shaanxi. Instead of being thin and straggly, they are wide and must be slurped and bitten off. The broth is so tangy and rich that just the smell of it brings tears to my eyes.

I thank my *sifu*, then we sit for a moment in silence. I'm not sure what I'm waiting for, but it quickly becomes obvious that Mr Zhang and Bai aren't allowed to give me any clues, and they're clearly expecting me to eat the noodles. The one thing I notice, before I pick up my chopsticks, is that this is not the usual china used at the Black Bamboo. Instead of the familiar white background and sketched outline of a bamboo plant, this bowl is patterned with intricate blue lotus flowers. I sense that, whatever I'm looking for, it has something to do with this dish.

I pick up my chopsticks, unwrap them from their paper, break the wooden halves apart, and tentatively pick up the first steaming noodle. The taste is good: rich and meaty. I set down the enormous noodle, pick up the spoon provided, and take a sip of the rich, salty broth. It's all delicious and piping hot. I burn my tongue a little, but there's nothing unusual about the noodles themselves, nor the broth. It all tastes as it should, as far as I can tell – no strange punch of cinnamon lurking in the flavours, no incongruous whack of liquorice that might be a clue to something else.

So, if the clue is not in the food itself, it must be hidden somewhere in the unusual serving bowl. I look round the surface of the dish again, taking in the blue and white hand-painted lotus designs. It's beautiful – but, again, there's nothing in particular for me to latch on to, no clue that I can see.

I start to eat the noodles again, faster this time, blowing on each bite quickly before I take it in. Again, I burn my tongue, and my eyes are still tearing up. My nose is running a little with the heat, and I consider blowing it on the cloth napkin, but decide to sniff instead. Mr Zhang picks up on this and hands me a clean tissue, which he seems to pull from thin air.

Time passes as I eat the noodles, the rest of the restaurant completely silent. Mr Zhang and Bai stay on the other side of the table, watching me eat my meal, almost as though I'm a messenger from a far-off land, who has come in from a long trek across Siberia and the Altay Mountains, and this is the meal that is being provided to me. I imagine myself kicking snow off my boots on the threshold, sitting down at the table and being presented with this meal. Not a bad reward.

It's a little disconcerting to be watched as you're eating a meal, though, but my mind is busy planning, fantasising and trying to guess what the clue will be.

Finally, I've eaten all the noodles and vegetables, and have drunk most of the broth. Murkily, through the shimmering oil on the surface of the broth, I can see something painted on the bottom of the bowl, but I can't quite make it out. Setting down my chopsticks and spoon, I take up the china dish in both hands, raise it to my lips, and drink down the last of the liquid in a single, long draught. I set the bowl down, wiping my lips on the napkin and blinking the tears out of my eyes. Perhaps it's my imagination, but Mr Zhang looks particularly focused on me at this moment.

I peer down into the bottom of the dish and see, among the blue lotus flowers, a single detail that does not appear elsewhere in the design. Right at the bottom, painted in the same blue and white as the flowers, is a number – 13.

There's no doubting it: this is the clue I'm looking for. There's nothing else it can be. Just as I raise my head to check with Mr Zhang and Bai, he says, 'Granddaughter, leave now.'

'What?' Bai looks appalled. 'But it's just getting interesting.'

'Time for bed,' he says firmly, and she shoots me a look of despair, before getting up from her seat and heading away from us. I can't help noticing that even her stroppy walk is graceful.

I can't wait any longer. 'It must be the number thirteen,' I say to Mr Zhang. 'That's it, isn't it? Thirteen?'

'Ah, but what does thirteen represent?'

I clench my fists. After cracking the coded email addresses, and heading over here in the middle of the night, I can't believe the test isn't over now that I've discovered the number.

I close my eyes and summon my mental filing system.

Thirteen
- 13
- Odd number
- Prime
- Superstition
- Bad luck

I shake my head.

'Look hard at the figures,' he instructs.

A thought strikes me. I stare into the dish at the figure 13 at the bottom, and imagine the 1 and 3 joining up.

'Is it – is it a letter B?'

I hold my breath for a second, worried I might have chosen the wrong thing. Then a wide smile breaks across Mr Zhang's face. He reaches for my hand and shakes it.

'Well done, Agatha. You remained calm under pressure. You kept your balance when everything around you was unbalanced. You have passed the second test of the Trial.'

He smiles again, and is that another wink?

By the time I get home, it's very late. Dad will be fast asleep, so I use the front door, rather than climb the tree.

When I get upstairs, I find Oliver on the floor in front of my door, curled up asleep. I have to step over him to get inside my room. I close the door and lean against it. It feels like many, many hours since I left. I've been out for a while, because it took time to walk to Soho, time to walk back – not to mention the time it took to complete the challenge. My room is dark and cold, because I'd left the skylight ajar so that I could get back in. The night air has cooled and seeped inside, chilling everything.

I climb on to my bed to close the skylight. Then I lie on my back. I start to shiver, so I kick off my shoes and crawl under the covers, still fully dressed. I'm exhausted but I feel elated. 'I did it, Mum!' I whisper to her, before falling asleep.

6.

THE FORGOTTEN UNDERGROUND

Someone is thumping on a wooden drum. No – on my skull. No – on my . . . door?

'Urgh . . .' I struggle to open my eyes and focus. 'Yeah?'

'Agatha, can I come in?'

'Yeah, I guess . . .'

Dad enters. He's already dressed in his head gardener clothes with the official Hyde Park logo on the dark-green polo shirt. He's holding something out to me. I squint at it. It's dark and . . .

'The phone, Agatha,' Dad says at last, realising I'm struggling.

'Oh . . . Thanks.' I take the phone and he leaves the room.

'Agatha?' Liam's voice comes down the line.

'*Urghhhh?*' I say.

'Agatha?' He sounds concerned.

Must . . . make . . . an . . . effort. 'Yep. Present and correct,' I say groggily. 'Or just present, at least.'

'Right . . . Are you OK? I tried you loads of times last night.'

'Did you? Sorry. I was otherwise engaged.'

'The second test?' he whispers.

'Can't talk here. It's not safe. You never know who's listening.'

'Can I come over?'

I squint at my bedside clock: 6:00.

'Really?'

'It's important. I'm already on my way – I'll be there in ten.'

'OK . . .' I try to put the phone down on my bedside table but there isn't room among the empty mugs and used plates, so I give up and put it on the floor. I drag myself to an upright position.

'Come on, girl: get yourself up and dressed,' I tell myself sternly. Luckily, no one is around to hear me, unless you count Oliver. He pricks up one ear, but otherwise ignores my strange behaviour. He is far too sleepy to care.

I lie there for another ten minutes before I finally make it out of bed. I have a quick wash, pull on my school uniform and run a brush through my bob. I catch sight of myself in the mirror. There are dark circles under my eyes. Finally, I drag myself downstairs. Liam is already in the kitchen, chatting with Dad. He catches my eye and smiles.

'Hello, lazybones.'

'Liam – it's ridiculously early!' Then I look at Dad. 'Is there anything to eat?' I watch him, gauging his mood. Has he had an email overnight, offering him the job?

'Sure – plenty. There's toast, cereal, eggs – anything you like, if you do it yourself.'

I study him through eyes that are dry and prickly from lack of sleep. He grabs his gardening gloves from the windowsill.

'Well, I'd best get to work – I've a lot to catch up on.'

Dad leaves and I start on breakfast. If Liam hadn't been here, I'd have asked Dad if he'd heard anything about Cornwall. I feel a pang at the thought that I'll have to wait until tonight now.

Liam pulls up a chair at the kitchen table while I fetch a bowl and plate and put some bread in the toaster. Then I take a seat opposite him.

'What was that about?' he asks.

I look up from pouring cornflakes into my bowl. 'What?'

'Your dad. There was a weird atmosphere between you.'

I hesitate. I'm not sure I want to talk to Liam about the possible move – it might make it real. He picks up on my uncertainty.

'It's all right – you don't have to tell me if you don't feel like it. Are you OK, though?'

I shrug. 'Been better. Look, do you mind if we change the subject?'

'Oh, yeah – did you get the second test?'

'I did, and I'll tell you about it later. How about you tell me what you found out, while I eat breakfast?'

'OK. Well, the sinkhole's right over a Tube line tunnel, the Waterloo and City line. I thought it might be important, seeing as you'd asked me to let you know what was underneath.'

I shovel in a mouthful of cereal and frown in concentration. The Waterloo and City line is a shuttle service, running between two stations: Waterloo (as you'd expect) and Bank, in the area of London known as the City (even though the whole of London is a city really). The trains don't stop at any other stations.

I finish my cereal, ignoring Liam's repeated demands for a reaction. At last, I put up a hand. 'Shhh. I'm thinking.'

'Right . . . Course you are . . .' He picks up the newspaper he brought with him from home and begins to flick through it. I put my bowl in the sink and check my watch. I haven't got time for toast.

'You got everything you need for school?' I ask him.

'Course.'

'Right, let's get going.'

He pushes back his chair and stands up. 'Where to?'

'The London Library. We need to do some research.'

'Surely it won't be open at this time?'

'Let me worry about that,' I say mysteriously.

'OK then. I'll pay for a taxi.'

I smile broadly for the first time this morning. 'That sounds good. Maybe I can snatch forty winks in the car.'

He hails a black cab on the main road, and we whizz over to the library in St James's Square, arriving far too quickly for my liking – I'm all cosy in the back of the cab, with my head on Liam's shoulder, when we arrive. We climb out of the taxi and Liam pays the driver through the window. He always has loads of cash on him. Liam's parents work overseas and have been in Hong Kong for the last few years, so he hardly ever sees them. I'd never say this to Liam, but I'd much rather live in a small cottage with my dad than in a grand flat without him, like Liam does.

We turn to survey the London Library building. The lights are all off and the front door looks very much closed and locked.

'It's shut,' Liam says.

'I know, but it'll be OK.' I tap on the door using a special sequence of knocks – a kind of code. It's actually a cha-cha rhythm, but I don't bother to explain. The doorman and his wife used to do ballroom dancing together.

There is the sound of movement from within, then various locks and bolts are audibly released. The door opens.

'Miss Agatha,' says Clive, the elderly doorman. He taps his cap in polite greeting.

'Mister . . .' I hesitate – 'Clive,' I say, at last, performing a small bow. Clive is rather stately and it always seems a bit rude just calling him by his first name, but he insists on it.

'And Master Liam – what a pleasure,' says Clive.

'Hi, Clive,' says Liam, less formally.

Clive glances around, like an illegal street trader checking for cops, then nods for us to enter.

'Thanks for letting us in,' I say.

'Any time, any time,' Clive says. He lowers his voice. 'Just don't tell anyone: I don't want to receive angry letters from jealous library lovers.'

Liam laughs. 'We won't – I promise.'

Clive hands me a key and we place our school backpacks in one of the lockers. Then he gestures towards the library stacks.

'Make yourselves at home,' he says.

'What are we looking for?' asks Liam as we head towards the stacks.

'Schematics for the Waterloo and City line. And any details of the abandoned British Museum Tube station.'

Liam groans. 'More plans – of course.'

'What did you think? That we were here to read Marvel comics?'

Liam brightens. 'Do they have those?'

I roll my eyes. 'I don't know, Liam. But that isn't what we're here for, OK?'

'No, you're right – the investigation must come first.'

I decide to overlook his robotic delivery of this statement.

We have a fair idea of the section we need from previous research sessions. It doesn't take long to find the plans relating to the Underground system. We scan the shelves.

'Waterloo and City line,' says Liam, pulling out a folder.

'Great! Now we just need to find anything on the British Museum station.'

That's not so easy. Whereas there's plenty of information regarding the stops that are in use, material on the out-of-service stations is trickier to find – if indeed there is any there at all.

At last, my eyes alight on a small hardback book, squeezed between various folders: *The Forgotten Underground: London's Secret Stations.* I take it from the shelf and join Liam, who is sitting at a table, working through the schematics of the Waterloo and City line.

I sit down next to him.

'What are we looking for?' he asks again.

'I'm not sure. I'm hoping we'll know it when we find it.'

I flick through the book – which doesn't seem to have an index (a real failing in any reference book, in my opinion) – searching for any reference to the British Museum stop. There are various maps and plans. I turn the book to study a landscape image of the lines going in and out of Bank station – and then I see it: there's a link from Bank to the defunct British Museum station.

Liam has got there as well at the same time – his finger is on the disused rail track showing on the much larger plans he's been studying. We catch one another's eye.

'What does it mean?' he asks.

'I don't know exactly. But I do know I need to investigate the sinkhole from underground, to see what's been going on down there.'

'That sounds like a terrible idea after that woman warned you off.'

I grin. 'You didn't really think I was going to listen to her, did you?'

He shakes his head sadly. 'I know you far too well for that.' He glances at his watch and lets out a yelp. 'Yikes, we have to get out of here – we're going to be late for school!'

Liam treats us to another cab – but this time we've hit rush hour. There's a lot more traffic on the roads, and the journey to St Regis is halting and frustrating. In the end, he pays the driver and we jog the last few hundred metres. Well – he jogs and I walk. Liam is a lot more intimidated by authority than I am and can't stand getting into trouble at school.

Mr Perkins is standing guard on the gate when we arrive, and Liam looks back over his shoulder at me, pleadingly.

'Please, Agatha, hurry up!'

I'm not being deliberately mean. I just don't want to arrive at school panting and covered in sweat.

By the time we make it into school, the corridors are empty.

'What do you reckon?' asks Liam. 'Form class or assembly?'

I put an ear to the hall door and hear Dr Hargrave

droning on about uniform, and how important it is to take pride in our appearance.

'They're all in there,' I whisper, pointing to the door.

So we wait outside the hall and just mingle with everyone as they come pouring out. Easy.

Brianna pushes her way through the throng. 'There you are,' she says. 'I hear you were in big trouble in form class – or would have been, if you'd been there.' She frowns. 'Except, if you *had* been there, you wouldn't have been in trouble, would you? Have you been to the office, to report your arrival?'

'Not yet,' says Liam, looking horror-struck. 'I'm going to get my first ever late mark,' he wails.

Brianna catches my eye and smirks.

'Don't be mean,' I tell her. 'He prides himself on his hundred per cent attendance record.'

'And now it's ruined,' says Liam sadly.

'At least you've not been told off about your appearance,' says Brianna. 'Hargrave caught me in the corridor on the way to assembly and told me I've got to dye my hair a "natural colour". I pointed out that blue *is* a perfectly natural colour – the sky, the sea . . .'

'How'd our esteemed headmaster take that?' I ask.

She shakes her head sadly. 'Not well. Not well at all.'

'Oh dear . . .'

'We'd better get over to the office,' says Liam.

We bid Brianna farewell and I allow him to propel me to the office at top speed. We are both reprimanded by the school secretary – although Liam's telling-off is rather more gentle than mine, as he is a model student.

'What lesson have you got now?' she asks us.

'Maths,' says Liam.

'Really?' I mutter. 'It's like I'm stuck in an eternal maths lesson. Maybe it's a metaphor for hell.'

'Well, off you go then,' says the secretary firmly.

Liam once again hurries me through the corridors. We arrive at the classroom and he goes straight in, holding the door open so I can follow.

'Mr Lau, Ms Oddlow, how nice of you to join us,' says Mr Patel, our maths teacher.

'Sorry, Mr Patel,' we murmur dutifully.

I spend the lesson using one portion of my little grey cells to do the calculations set by Mr Patel – and the remainder to ruminate on the case in hand. By lunchtime, I'm wondering how I've ever survived a full school day – it's so long! And tedious. I catch up with Liam and Brianna at Exile Island – the table in the canteen only occupied by weird kids like us (except nobody is quite like us . . .).

'Agatha – are you with us?' asks Brianna.

'Sorry?'

'You were really giving Sarah the evil eye,' she says.

'Oops! I hadn't realised.'

'Haven't you got PE with her later?'

My heart sinks. Lacrosse – out on the field, with studded boots and those lethal sticks with the cages on top. And Sarah Rathbone.

'I'll have to plead injury of some sort,' I say, in desperation.

'You'll never get away with it,' says Brianna. 'Doughty made Fiona Lewis do netball with a broken leg last year.'

'I don't think that can be right . . .' says Liam, cutting in.

'Just ask Fiona!' says Brianna. 'She was limping about like a rabbit that'd been caught in a trap.'

'I still think . . .' tries Liam.

'Look – there she is!' says Brianna. 'Let's ask her. Fiona! Hey – Fiona!'

Fiona Lewis, a lanky girl with long red hair, which she hates and everyone else envies, stops with her tray. 'What's up?'

'Tell them about Doughty and your broken leg.'

Fiona rolls her eyes. 'It's true – she made me do netball. It was a complete farce. I can't play at the best of times! You should've seen me, hopping about the court and trying not to fall over. It hurt like hell as well.'

She walks off, and Brianna turns to Liam,

'Now do you believe me?'

He's turned pale. 'Sometimes I worry about this place.'

'What am I going to do?' I wail. 'She'll kill me.'

'Who? Doughty?' says Liam.

'Keep up!' says Brianna. 'She's talking about Sarah.'

'Ohhhh . . .' He pulls a face. 'Maybe she'll be in a good mood – first week back and all that.'

'Right. And maybe she helps out at a homeless shelter in her spare time,' says Brianna.

'I'm dead,' I wail.

'I think you are,' says Brianna.

I barely survive PE. Sarah Rathbone has clearly rounded up all her cronies, and every girl on the field seems to be running straight at me. Miss Doughty doesn't notice, as always – I'm not gifted at sport, so I'm invisible. By the time Sarah sticks out her foot and trips me, I'm almost grateful. Despite the warm summer we've had, the ground is soft with moss and I'm tempted to close my eyes and let the game go thundering on above and around me. But then a foot kicks me in the belly and I realise I need to get up, now.

I limp off – still ignored by Doughty – and head

for the office, to have my injuries tended to. But 'tended to' always involves them applying a sticking plaster and sending you back to class.

I make it through domestic science, in which the felt rabbit I'm making is beginning to resemble Darth Vader. Liam keeps leaning over and whispering, 'I *am* your father,' and I can't stop giggling.

At last, at ten past four, the bell goes for the end of the day, and I limp home. My shins are coated in mud, and I'm pretty sure there's some more stuck behind my ears.

Liam walks out of the school gates with me. 'Good luck getting the mud off,' he calls as he heads towards his bus stop.

Dad is still at work when I get back, and I take a warm shower, letting the water wash over my scratches and scrapes. Who would have thought a game of lacrosse could be so savage? Probably anyone who's ever played it, I decide. I try not to think about what might be coming later this evening – an announcement from Dad to say he's been offered the job.

I dry myself and go up to my room, where I pull on a navy stripe slash-neck top and capri-length dark-blue jeans. I tie a red silk scarf round my neck and take a seat at my desk. I need a distraction, so I've decided to go through everything I know so far – all my observations and discoveries on the museum murder, the disused station and the Waterloo and City line. I open my laptop and keep Googling for additional information – anything Liam or I might have missed.

When all my research draws a blank, I turn to the Guild Trial. So far, I have the letters A and B. Not a lot to go on. Apart from being the start of the alphabet, the two letters don't immediately bring anything substantial to mind. I grab the dictionary and read through words that start with *Ab* – there's 'absolute', 'abysmal', 'abracadabra', but nothing that leaps out at me.

I'm so engrossed, I haven't even noticed that more than three hours have gone by. I jump when Dad calls up to me at around half past eight.

'Agatha, I'm back. Can you come down here, please?'

I guess this is where I find out if we're leaving London.

I walk down the two flights of stairs super slowly, putting off the knowledge for as long as possible.

It reminds me of a thought experiment called Schrödinger's cat. A scientist (Schrödinger) said you can put a cat in a box with a flask of poison. As long as you don't open the box, you have no way of knowing for sure if the cat has been poisoned. So, in a way, the cat is both alive and dead at the same time. In the same way, as long as I don't 'open the box', I'm both moving to Cornwall and staying in London.

At the bottom of the stairs, I find Dad waiting.

'You're back late,' I say.

'I had a lot to do. It's peak season for weeds, and I had to catch up after taking time off for the interviews.' He points to the living room. 'Let's go in here,' he says.

I walk ahead of him and sit on the edge of the sofa, where I start biting my nails, before I remember about the painted stars. Dad takes a seat on the armchair, which is at right angles to the sofa.

'Dad, before you say anything . . .' I start, just as he says, 'Look, Aggie, the last thing I want is for you to be unhappy . . .'

I wave my hand to stop him. 'Look, I'm sorry, Dad. I just got a shock when you suddenly started talking about the new job, and moving to Cornwall and everything. I reacted badly.'

He looks down at the floor and says, 'So, now you're over the shock, how do you feel about it?'

I feel as though I've received a painful electric shock to my chest. 'Is it definite? Did you take the job?'

He looks up in surprise. 'Of course not! I'd never do that without checking with you.'

'But you've been offered it?' I prompt.

He nods.

'That's great, Dad.'

'Thanks, love. So . . . would you be OK with it? With moving to Cornwall?'

'I'm not sure. I mean, I'm really pleased for you

and everything. It's just . . . I'm sorry – it's still a lot to process. It's just leaving Brianna and Liam, and this house and everything . . .'

'I get it,' he says. 'Let's take a while to think it through, shall we?' He gets up. 'You must be starving. Omelettes all right?'

'Sounds great. Isn't it my turn?'

'No, you're all right. I've got this.'

I stay in the living room, trying to work out if I could be happy somewhere else – if I could settle into a new home in a place that didn't have Liam or Brianna or Mum's grave. My list still has only two points in favour of moving to Cornwall: more sunshine, less pollution. I'll have to find the time to come up with more pros. After a while, Oliver pushes his way into the room and rubs against my legs. I scoop him up and he settles in my lap, purring loudly.

'Ugh, Oliver! You stink of sardines!' He butts his head against my hand in ecstasy, oblivious to my reproof. 'What am I going to do, boy?' I ask him. 'I have to finish the Guild Trial – there's still one test to come. And there's the museum investigation as well – something's definitely going on with that disused station.' Oliver mews in agreement, which feels oddly comforting.

At last, Dad calls me into the kitchen for dinner. I gently lift the cat from my lap, and place him in the warm spot I'm vacating. He lets out a plaintive 'Meow', but turns round twice and falls asleep almost immediately.

My omelette is cheese and baked beans – a special combination I came up with a few years ago. I don't feel much like eating, though. I stare at the food on my plate, while Dad makes small talk about the park, and how two of the gardeners are getting married. I really like both of them, but I can't feel much pleasure for them just now.

Dad is looking at me expectantly, so I say, 'That's nice.'

He nods enthusiastically. 'They're going to have the photos in the park – won't that be lovely?'

'That's nice,' I say again.

There's a long pause, then he says, 'I only want what's best for you, Agatha – you do know that, don't you?'

I nod and try to smile, but a tear plops on to my plate instead. 'I'm sorry,' I say. 'Do you mind if I eat this later?'

'Of course not, Aggie.'

'Thanks, Dad.'

I almost run from the room. I hate feeling so miserable over something that should be a wonderful opportunity for Dad. Why can't I just feel happy for him?

When I get to the second floor, I push open my door and freeze on the threshold. My room is full of snakes. On instinct, I step back and shut the door again. I stand in front of it at the top of the stairs, my heart pounding. *Snakes!* How on earth did they get there? Obviously, someone's been in my room. What if he or she is still in there?

I should get Dad. But curiosity overtakes me. I take a few deep breaths and push the door open, slowly. I can't see anyone inside. My heart calms as I run through the possibilities.

Of course, this might be a threat – but it could be the Gatekeepers' Guild, setting the third and final test of the Trial. I stand very still and squint at the nearest reptile. It has something painted in white on its back.

So this *is* almost certainly a test. The Guild wouldn't put dangerous animals in my bedroom – I'm sure of that. To be on the safe side, I try to work out what sort of snakes they are. With my eyes closed, I Change Channel, conjuring up images of British serpents – grass and viper. The grass snake, although it can be very large – reaching up to 1.3 metres in length – is harmless. The viper, also known as the adder, is smaller (75cm maximum) and venomous, with a warning zigzag along its back.

I open my eyes to stare more closely, and see – with more than a little relief, if I'm honest – that there are no such markings. These are not poisonous creatures. In fact, with their compact size and golden skin, they're not snakes at all. No – despite their flicking tongues and snake-shape bodies, these are a type of legless lizard, called a slow-worm, and therefore completely harmless.

Reassured and relieved, I step inside and close the door, careful where I put my feet. I put on gloves – I've heard that the touch of a warm-blooded body can burn reptiles, though I don't know if this is actually true – and pick up one of the lizards. It has a letter and a smaller number painted on its back.

All thoughts of Cornwall vanish at the thrill of receiving the final part of the Trial. I empty the owl pellets from the Perspex box and place the lizards inside, one at a time, noting each letter in my notebook. Then I check there are none behind the bookcase or beneath my bed. As I'm lying on my stomach on the floor, Dad knocks on the door.

'Agatha, are you all right?'

'I'm fine,' I call back.

'Can I come in?'

'Now's not a great time,' I say, gently taking hold of a slow-worm that's making rapid progress towards the space beneath my bed.

'I'll give you a bit more alone time, but let me know if you want to chat later.'

'OK. Thanks.'

I hear him going back downstairs. I place the final slow-worm in the box, and then I sit at my desk and stare at the letters and numbers on their backs. At first, I assume it's just a straightforward anagram, in which I have to rearrange the letters according to the sequence indicated by the numbers. Some of the lizards have only a number without a letter, so these must represent spaces. This gives me:

$$^1G\ ^2Y\ ^3M\ ^4J\ ^5-\ ^6Y\ ^7-\ ^8F\ ^9C\ ^{10}Y\ ^{11}G\ ^{12}-\ ^{13}G\ ^{14}C$$
$$^{15}-\ ^{16}G\ ^{17}X\ ^{18}J\ ^{19}-\ ^{20}Q\ ^{21}W\ ^{22}P\ ^{23}Y\ ^{24}R\ ^{25}Z$$

GYMJ Y FCYG GC GXJ QWPYRZ? That clearly isn't right. That's when I realise there's another layer to the clue – it's a cipher, and I need to work out what form of encryption has been used before I can crack it.

At first I try a simple Caesar cipher, in which the entire alphabet moves one or more spaces forward or backward – so A becomes C, B becomes D, C becomes E, for instance. I attempt to decode it in this fashion for about half an hour, but this gets me nowhere. At last, I accept that what I have is a random cipher, in which each letter has been randomly allocated a counterpart, with no pattern to the coding. The only way to decode a cipher like this is by trial, error and logic.

I study the message. I know that the only two single-letter words in the English language are 'I' and 'a' (unless you count 'o', which is old-fashioned and only used in poetry). I assume the Y on its own in the cipher must equal 'a', because it's unlikely that 'I' will appear in a formal message. Then I figure that the three-letter word, 'GXJ', is most likely to be either 'the', 'and' or 'you'. I try 'the' first, which would mean G stands for T. This gives me four letter Ts, all of which look likely. It also gives me two letter Es, which again seem correctly placed. I carry on in this way, partly through trial and error, and partly through my knowledge of frequently occurring letters, and where they are most likely to appear in words. At last, I have the following code frame:

Y = A	M = K
F = B	P = L
Z = D	R = N
J = E	C = O
X = H	W = S
Q = I	G = T

The end result is the following message:

TAKE A BOAT TO THE ISLAND.

Picking up the box of slow-worms, I head back down the first flight of stairs to where Dad keeps his keys. I grab the set I'll need if my instincts are correct, then I go down to the ground floor. Dad has the telly turned up, watching some thriller about plants taking over the world. It figures – he'd probably prefer a world in which plants were in charge.

'Just popping out into the park for a short time,' I call to Dad.

'What?' he shouts back.

'Just going out. Back soon!' I leave at once, before Dad can spot me with the box of reptiles. Outside, I empty the box into some thick undergrowth in the park. I don't remember Dad ever mentioning slow-worms in Hyde Park, but hopefully they'll survive. Then I begin to run.

Within moments, I'm at the boathouse beside the Serpentine, where the boats for hire are stored. Manny, who runs the place, has gone for the day, but Dad's keys gain me access to the boats. I throw open one of the shed doors and examine the array of painted wooden rowing boats inside. I pick a small one and drag it out of the shed by its rope.

It's past ten o'clock and getting dark, but I pull the boat down to the edge of the lake and climb inside. Then I start to row. I'm quite a good rower: Manny often lets me take a boat for free in the holidays when there aren't too many customers, so I've had a lot of practice. As I get near to the island that sits in the middle of the Serpentine, I see a strange glow, like the lamp of a giant glow-worm – a glow-worm being a type of beetle. (Why do so many things have 'worm' as part of their name when they are really no such thing?)

On closer inspection, there's a single lantern hanging from a bush. Its light feels like a friend in the now slightly eerie darkness. It also confirms that I interpreted the latest instruction correctly – the lamp must have been placed here to guide me. Despite this reassurance, it's very quiet here on the island, and there is a chill in the air. I could be miles from humanity, and I shiver at my sudden sense of isolation and vulnerability. Then I push away thoughts of things that go bump in the night, and instead throw the boat-rope over the mooring post and climb out.

Walking towards the lantern, I see that it illuminates a single envelope fixed by a pin to a bamboo cane. As I unstick it from its post, I inspect the paper. It's of the same high-quality paper as before, so it definitely is the Gatekeepers who've brought me here. I place it in my pocket and row back, being sure to return the boat to its original position, and locking the boathouse carefully behind me.

Back at Groundskeeper's Cottage, the TV has been

turned off. I find Dad in the kitchen, tapping his fingers on the table. He jumps up as I enter.

'Where have you been? Have you seen the time?'

'Just into the park. I thought that would be all right. I found a slow-worm in my room and I wanted to release it safely. I'm sorry – I didn't mean to scare you.'

Dad is distracted by this information. 'A slow-worm? Up in the attic?'

I nod. 'I was going to ask you how you think it got up there, but you were watching telly.'

He thinks for a moment. 'It must have been inside something you were carrying.'

'That makes sense,' I say, happy not to have to lie to him.

His face softens. 'You should have asked me. I don't like you going into the park late at night.'

'Sorry. I'll ask next time.'

He kisses me on the top of my head. 'I'll say goodnight, love. We've both had quite a long day. You need to get to bed.'

'OK. Night, Dad.'

I go upstairs, slip his keys back on to their rack, then head up to my room, where I sit down at my desk and tear open the envelope. It contains a sheet of paper with some things written on it.

First, there is a circle. I place the paper beside the sheet bearing the letter A and close my eyes for a moment to bring up the image of the figure 13 from the noodle bowl that represented B . . . Maybe this isn't a circle, but a letter – O. So then I have A, B and O.

Beneath the O are some words: *Give and take*.

At the very bottom of the page, a line of text reads: *You have until midnight*.

I check my watch – five past eleven. I feel the pulse in my temple speed up. I don't have much time.

ABO could stand for almost anything . . . It could just mean 'boa' – and I could visit London Zoo to see the boa constrictors . . . But the letters were delivered in the order ABO, so I continue to reflect. There's an Association of British Orchestras, but I can't see how that helps. There's a mountain pass in New Mexico called Abo Canyon – but surely the

Guild wouldn't expect me to travel there during term time . . .?

Give and take. Give and take. What do you give and take? Presents? Compromises? *ABO . . . Give and take . . .*

Suddenly I understand.

I grab my backpack in case I need any of my gadgets and put my beret on my head. Then I climb out through the skylight and down the tree. It's now quarter past eleven – I hope I'm in time.

The West End Donor Centre on Margaret Street is the biggest blood donation clinic in all of London. I take a bus, which is empty – bar a drunk man right at the back, who mumbles to himself the whole way and ignores me, thank goodness, and a stressed-looking mother clutching a whimpering baby. I hop off at the closest stop to Margaret Street. The donor centre looks very closed when I get there. However, there's a light shining out from one small window, so I knock gently on the pane. A moment later, a uniformed nurse appears at the front door.

'We're closed,' she says.

'Yes, but . . . I have an appointment.'

She narrows her eyes. 'What is the name?'

'Oddlow. Agatha Oddlow.'

She consults a sheet and shakes her head.

'Felicity Lemon?' I try.

She nods. 'Come in.'

I follow her into the clinic. She leads me down empty white corridors and through double doors into identical empty white corridors. There's something disconcerting about a hospital environment out of hours. Too many thrillers have been set in just such a place, where an evil doctor attempts some illegal operation to incapacitate the hero or heroine.

What if I've got it all wrong? What if I've walked straight into a trap?

'Where are we going?' I ask the nurse's back as she strides ahead, but she doesn't respond. Too late now . . .

Finally, we reach the end of a corridor, and the

nurse raps on the door of a doctor's office. She opens the door and nods for me to enter. My palms are sweating by the time I step inside, unsure whether I'll encounter a friend or a foe.

And then I'm looking straight into the smiling face of Professor D'Oliveira.

7.

NEW GIRL

I'm breathless with the realisation of what has happened, so I stand there for a long moment. Did you know that a 'moment' used to be equivalent to ninety seconds? This would mean a moment can't really be long or short. It feels as though a fizzy bottle of Coke has been opened somewhere in my chest, and the bubbles are effervescing through my veins, fizzing and popping and foaming up into my brain. I've done it, I've succeeded, and, like my mother, I'm about to become a member of the Gatekeepers' Guild.

And, perhaps, I will finally find out what happened to her.

The professor stands up and walks over, smiling. She holds out something to me and I extend my hand to accept it. The object is very small. It's a badge made of gold, and – carefully wrought in the metal – is the symbol of the Guild: a tiny key.

'Well, Agatha Oddlow – you did it. You did it, child!'

She puts her arms round me in a quick hug, and I can barely believe that I'm getting a hug from the professor. Not that she is cold or uncaring, but she is usually very . . . professional. Mostly I have to make do with a small smile, or a nod, or a pleased tone of voice. This is quite new. I'm not sure how comfortable I am with both the professor and Mr Zhang behaving differently from usual.

'Thank you,' I say. It sounds a bit weak, but nothing could sum up the mixture of emotions I'm experiencing right now.

She turns to the nurse who brought me in. *Of course*, I realise, *this is not a nurse at all, but another Guild member in uniform.*

'Agatha, I'd like to introduce you to Sofia Solokov.

Until a moment ago, she was the youngest member of the Guild, in its entire history. I'm afraid to say, Sofia, that your record has just been broken.'

I turn to look at the girl who has stepped up beside me. She has long black hair tied back in a ponytail and is observing me out of dark, glittering eyes. She does not look pleased.

'Congratulations.' The word sounds anything but congratulatory.

Sometimes you just know that you're not going to get on with someone. I had this feeling immediately when I met Sarah Rathbone, before she'd even said anything. Although we've only been in each other's presence for a few minutes, I already know that I'm not going to get on with Sofia Solokov.

The professor continues. 'Sofia is just nineteen, but she is a full agent already, as she's completed her training. You still have to do that. So I think there could be no better role model for you than Sofia.'

I mumble something in agreement, but I'm not ready for what comes next.

'And that is why I have assigned the task of

mentoring you to Sofia. She will be responsible for training you, looking after you, and inducting you into the Guild. If you have any questions, direct them to her first.'

I freeze. This is not welcome news. I had assumed, since Professor D'Oliveira was my main contact for the Guild, the person who I always spoke to, that she would be my mentor. Not to mention the fact that she was my mother's mentor. Why won't she be training me? Before I can say anything, the professor picks up on the sense of surprise I can't keep from crossing my face as I look between her and Sofia.

'I am an old woman, Agatha. You need a more energetic mentor. Ms Solokov will be a much better match for you.'

I can't say I'm pleased with this turn of events, but I push it to the back of my mind. I've got the thing that I most wanted – access to the Guild's file rooms in a secret bunker deep under London. Using that, I can find out all about Mum. It's this that I address immediately.

'Professor, I know that I only just passed; I know

that there will be a lot of other things to do, but . . . is there any chance I can visit the file rooms?'

The professor smiles a little sadly. 'I am afraid, Agatha, that you are setting too much store by what is in your mother's files. You will not bring her back by finding out more about her life in the Guild.'

'I know that, but . . . maybe there's something that will explain what happened to her?' I look the professor in the eye. 'You know she didn't die in a bike accident, or her bike wouldn't have been immaculate afterwards.'

The professor blushes slightly. Then she nods. 'You are right. You do understand, however, that anything you find in the files remains the property of the Gatekeeepers' Guild?'

'Of course – I promise not to take anything.'

'Nor to share any information with anyone external to the Guild – even your father?'

I hesitate, but my desire to know the truth wins out. 'I promise.'

There's a noise from Sofia at my shoulder, a sort of 'Hmph'.

'Yes, Sofia? Do you have something to say?'

'It's just that, Professor, new recruits aren't usually given the freedom of the file rooms . . .'

My eyes snap round to look at Sofia, and I can't keep the look of anger out of them.

She narrows her eyes at me, as though in challenge.

'No, you are right, Sofia, we do not normally give recruits the run of the file rooms,' the professor says.

My heart sinks and my hands clench involuntarily at my sides.

'However,' she goes on, 'we are not allowing Agatha the freedom to wander willy-nilly through the file rooms – she will be chaperoned by the two of us.'

I breathe a sigh of relief. The professor starts to walk, and I follow her. We go through a door at the back of the office, into a corridor, through several fire doors and into a part of the building that doesn't seem to be maintained by anyone until we get to a small lift door set into a concrete wall. The professor fumbles around in her pockets for a minute, then pulls out a small key, which she inserts into a panel.

When she turns it, a light comes on behind the down-arrow button. She presses the button, and there's a gentle whirr from behind the door as the lift starts to ascend towards us.

I want to say something, to have some sort of conversation, for politeness' sake. But with Sofia there, and with my mind so fixed on where I'm about to go, I can't think of a single thing to say. It would seem banal to talk about the weather as we're set to descend into the secret depths of the Guild's headquarters under London.

The lift arrives, there's a ping, and the metal doors slide open. The cubicle inside is dusty, and can scarcely have been used since it was installed. We step in, the doors close, and the lift begins what turns out to be a very long descent. I've read that there are some skyscrapers in the world, such as the Burj Khalifa in Dubai or the One World Trade Center in New York, that have such incredibly fast and efficient lifts that you'd barely know you'd travelled hundreds of metres in a matter of seconds.

This is not one of those lifts.

It rumbles and rattles for a good thirty seconds before my ears pop once, then twice, and we keep going down, down, down. It's weird to think I had no idea this was here – that I've passed by the blood donor centre a hundred times or more, without realising the building held this secret access to the world of the Gatekeepers.

After about two minutes have passed, my ears pop one last time, then the lift seems to slow. It rattles, judders, and then comes to a bumpy stop.

The doors open.

We're in a dimly lit corridor, recognisable to me as the work of the Guild, but not an area that I've visited before.

'Come along then,' the professor says, marching forward with her walking stick.

Sofia and I walk deferentially behind her, and I catch Sofia glancing sideways at me. There's something familiar about her, I realise now. I didn't catch it when I first met her, dressed in her nurse's uniform, and I didn't catch it with the surprise of discovering that she was a Guild agent.

But it's *something* nevertheless.

Have I met her before? Did she used to go to St Regis – someone I remember from my early days there? Or someone I might have seen in old photographs of the school? She looks like she might have been good at games – running and jumping, hitting balls with a stick across a field, and whacking people in the shins along the way. It's not inconceivable that she might feature in some of the photographs of the lacrosse team from a few years ago, or else the polo team, galloping around the country to bring glory to St Regis.

I file it away for now, because there are more important things afoot. We march down several corridors, and pass through several doors, each one of which the professor opens with a different key. Finally, she opens a door with her Guild key, and we step into a small corridor which smells of paraffin and grease. As we enter, Sofia closes the door behind us, and lights come on, stretching down the tunnel, and I can see what is in front of us.

It's a tiny miniature railway. I've ridden on these before – at fairs, when I was younger – but I didn't expect to see one down here. It looks out of place in the sober concrete passage. The professor strides forward and, rather awkwardly, lowers herself until she is straddling the miniature steam engine, fiddling with the dials and valves until I see a blue flame erupt in the engine's firebox, and steam start to wisp and curl from the funnel.

Sofia marches over and sits down, astride one of the 'carriages', reeling in her long legs until her feet are perched neatly on the side plates.

She gives me a hard stare, one eyebrow raised. 'Are you always going to be this slow?' she snipes. I purse my lips and stride over, swing my leg over the carriage two behind hers, and take hold.

'Here we go!' the professor calls as the engine chuffs into life and we start to move forward.

It seems incredibly slow to begin with, and I wonder why on earth they bothered to put it here. Even at the professor's slower pace, we could be walking faster than this. But then we start to pick up speed, more and more, and the acceleration goes on far longer than I could have anticipated.

The rails underneath us – each of which is barely thicker than a chocolate bar – start to rattle in an alarming manner. The walls of the tunnel begin to blur, and air whips my hair around my face and stings my eyes. I grip on tightly to the carriage, trying to tuck myself down against the wind. I'm careful to pitch my body right or left as the engine hurtles forward, navigating bends. We go through a maze of winding tunnels, and, as uncomfortable as the ride is, I can't deny the excitement of travelling at speed through this underground world. I think about how long it would have taken to travel this distance on foot.

Finally, seeing a red light in the distance, the professor applies the brakes to begin our deceleration. There's a screech of metal. The rattle of the rails gives one last kick, like the end of a spin cycle, and we coast to a stop in front of a set of broad stone steps leading up to an imposing door.

The professor chuckles as she rises stiffly from her seat.

'I always love doing that – to be honest, I only

picked the donation centre as the solution so I could get a chance to drive the train.'

She grins at me. And I grin back. I'm reminded that while I've become caught up in my need to learn the truth about Mum, there's also a lot of fun to be had as a member of the Guild. I'm looking forward to getting to know all about it. Sofia doesn't look quite so impressed.

We step up to the door, which is big and black with a silver knocker set into the centre. It looks like the kind of entryway you might see in Downing Street or Buckingham Palace – an official, serious door. I won't be surprised if there are armed guards positioned behind it.

The professor doesn't take out a key this time, but raps briskly on the silver knocker, steps back a pace, and waits. Though there's no visible peephole, there must be some kind of CCTV watching us, because, after a moment's wait, we hear the sound of bolts unlocking and bars sliding, and then the black portal opens, admitting a bright shaft of light into the tunnel. It momentarily dazzles me.

I glance over to see the professor and Sofia holding their hands up to their eyes, shielding themselves from the glare.

A voice comes from behind the door: 'Good afternoon, Professor.'

I take in the figure standing sentinel behind the door. I was quite right – the man has a service pistol and an extendable truncheon at his belt. Round his back, I glimpse what looks like a Taser and a canister of teargas.

Much of the underground network that I've explored has been completely unprotected. I suppose it would be impractical to have someone patrolling every tunnel, every door, every lift shaft and staircase to the surface. Instead, they rely on solid doors, well-maintained locks, and keys like my own, which seem to hold some secret, because one very simple key unlocks an enormous array of doors. Liam says he thinks it has to do with some kind of microchip, and that we might find out more if we put it through an X-ray scanner, but I can't bear the thought of damaging Mum's key in any way, so we never have.

In any case, this door is clearly too important *not* to be guarded.

We step forward, into the light, and our feet sink into a plush carpet. Stretching out in front of us is a corridor lined with the same elaborately woven floral carpet. There are chandeliers hanging from the ceiling, and down each side of the corridor are a number of doors, each set in an ornate frame.

I can't believe I'm back here at last – in the hallowed headquarters of the Gatekeepers' Guild. My mum was here. I picture her striding along the wood-panelled passageway. That is how I remember her – purposeful and focused. And laughing – she laughed a lot. Whatever is hidden in those files, it must take me at least a step closer to understanding how and why she died. What was she working on that got her into such terrible trouble?

The door closes behind us, and I jerk out of my reverie. I notice that the guard who let us in has a counterpart on the other side of the doorframe too. He doesn't say anything to us, but Dorothy and Sofia hand over identification cards, and Dorothy explains that I'm attending as her guest. The second guard, the one who hasn't spoken, escorts us down the corridor, past the dozen or so unmarked doors, until we get to the right one, and are shown into another grand corridor.

In yet more silence we walk through a maze of these corridors, and, after a while, I wonder how anyone can possibly know which way they're going. All the way, I'm drawing a map in my head, to call up again later, but it would only take me along the route that we've taken – there are countless other doors and corridors leading in all directions.

Left, left, right, left, right, right, left, straight ahead, left again . . .

I notice the professor glancing sideways at me, with something of a smile on her face, judging my reaction to all of this. She must realise how overwhelming it is. Of course, I know that the organisation's agents are codebreakers and lovers of puzzles in general, so in a way all of this makes sense. Having an exceptional, even photographic, memory, is almost a prerequisite for a Gatekeeper.

At last, still in complete silence, we arrive at our destination – a door unlike the myriad others we've already passed. It's bigger, for a start, and has an elaborate locking system on it, controlled by some sort of panel with switches to the right of the door. There are two more guards on this door, more heavily armed than the ones we've seen so far, and another guard sits at the console, presumably operating the locks.

Except for the guards, we've seen nobody in this labyrinth up till now, but here there's a small queue waiting to enter. We have to leave our bags in lockers and then walk through scanners to make sure we aren't carrying phones or cameras. The guards check the identification cards of everyone in the queue, taking particular care to verify the professor's story about me – and then, upon some sort of signal to the guard at the console, the door is unlocked with a mechanical whirring sound and a click. It hinges open and we all walk inside the astonishing file rooms.

The first time I glimpsed the Guild archives was also the first time I had really explored underground.

I'd taken a bike ride under the capital with Liam, exploring the maze of tunnels in our quest to discover what was causing the plague of red slime that was coming out of the taps all over London. We'd spied these massive rooms filled with files, and had stood for a while in awe, watching men and women going about their daily jobs in complete secrecy.

Even though I knew this room existed, there is something completely bizarre about the situation. How can all these people act like it's perfectly normal to be all the way down here beneath London? What do they tell their families about what they do and where they work? It's nearly midnight, but they're all behaving as if it's just an ordinary library in the middle of the day.

They scurry between the record files, flicking through cabinets filled with meticulously labelled brown folders. They take some out, they replace others, they carry files and individual pieces of paper off to one of the little low-walled cubicles at the side of the room, where there's a desk, a green glass reading lamp and a wooden chair. If you want to examine the files, it seems, you have to do so in the room, and in plain view of everyone else.

Another glance at the ceiling confirms my suspicion that the whole place is under CCTV surveillance. The professor, Sofia and I walk into the room, along with a small group of people who were waiting at the door with us. The others go off into the stacks, bearing notes, so that they can find the files they need. Clearly all of them already know what they're looking for, and are familiar with the geography of the room.

The professor takes us over to a desk where several archive assitants are seated at computer terminals. The computers look too modern in a room where everything has been typed and filed the old-fashioned way. Why haven't they filed their archives electronically? I wonder whether they feel it's too easy to hack the firewall of a computer system and much harder to infiltrate a physical file room that has real-life armed guards outside?

The professor addresses one of the archive assistants: 'Hello, yes, I would like to find a particular file . . .'

The assistant, a girl not much older than Sofia, wearing dangling, sparkly earrings and enormous half-moon glasses, smiles brightly at the professor.

'Well, that's what I'm here for!' She beams. 'Which file do you need?'

'I want to access the material on one of our previous agents.'

The girl types something at her computer terminal, then asks: 'And which agent is it?'

'Clara Oddlow.'

The girl looks up sharply, and all trace of her smile has been wiped from her face. She glances from the professor to me, and some sort of understanding seems to dawn in her expression.

'Oh, right, y-yes . . .' she stammers, typing the words on her keypad.

There's a lump in my throat which stops me from saying anything. The archive assistant swallows, looking at her screen, then takes a slip of paper from a stack at her desk and notes down a file reference, which she hands to the professor.

'Just down that way, about fifteen stacks.' She

points off to her left, towards a far corner of the room.

'Many thanks,' the professor says briskly.

We walk on, through the hush of the vast, thickly carpeted room.

I follow the professor, with Sofia behind me. It's a bit like being a prisoner escorted by guards. I'm trembling at the thought that soon I will have access to the cases Mum worked on before she died. Will the details of her death be in the files? I still don't know if the professor knows what happened, or only – like me – that Mum didn't die in a bike accident. I haven't had the courage to ask her. I'm aware of the blood pounding loudly in my ears. After we've walked for about thirty seconds, I realise I can no longer hear the tip-tap of computer keyboards back at the archive assistants' desk.

Professor D'Oliveira doesn't glance more than once at the piece of paper she's been given, but soon we are standing in front of a filing cabinet, and – using another tiny key from one of her series of keyrings – she is unlocking the cabinet and sifting through the folders within.

My heart is beating fast. The label on the drawer reads EXPIRED – does this mean expired cases or expired agents? It seems a bit cold, if it's referring to agents who died in the line of duty. As the professor's fingers flick expertly through the folders, I can read the tags on some of them, each bearing a single name. Some of the files are as thick as a biology textbook, others so thin that they can't contain more than one or two sheets of paper.

As the professor's fingers settle on a file, and I read CLARA ODDLOW, my mother's name, on the front, my heart rate kicks up another notch. I can feel myself sweating. I'm not in danger, I'm not being chased through a tunnel or threatened with a gun, yet I feel more scared now than I have in a very long time – perhaps since the day that I lost Mum, and realised Dad and I were all alone in the world.

The professor pulls out the file and turns to me. 'Are you ready?'

'Yes . . .' I say, uncertainly.

'Are you sure?' she asks gently, putting a hand on my shoulder.

Either out of some desire to give us privacy, or because she can't stand this display of sentimentality, Sofia turns and walks a little way down the row of filing cabinets. There she stops, as if standing sentry.

'Yes,' I say, more certain this time. 'Yes, I'm sure – I've been waiting a long time for this. Dad and I both deserve to know the truth.'

The professor smiles. 'Spoken like the true daughter of Clara.' She turns serious. 'But don't forget the promise you made about confidentiality – we'll have to talk later about what exactly you can share with your father.'

She hands me the file, which is a thick one, clearly bulging with information.

I place it on top of the filing cabinet, take a deep breath, and flip open the cover of my mother's file.

The first piece of paper in the file is blank. It must be some kind of cover sheet. I turn it over. The next piece of paper is also blank. I turn it over. I turn the next one over too, and the next . . .

They're all blank.

Looking for some kind of explanation, I turn to the professor.

'What . . .?' I say. No other words come.

But the professor is just shaking her head. 'No, it can't be . . .' She looks panicked, stricken almost.

Sofia quickly comes back over to where we are standing. 'What? What is it?' she asks in her brusque tone.

I demonstrate by riffling through all the blank pieces of paper in my mother's file.

'The notes,' the professor says, 'they've been wiped. The pages are all blank.'

'There must be a mistake,' Sofia says.

There's a screeching in my head, the beginning of a high-pitched scream. It wants to burst out, to break the silence in this awful quiet room.

I have a realisation, and clutch at it like I'm drowning and it's my only salvation. 'This is part of the Trial, right?' I say. 'I haven't passed yet after all, have I? This is another challenge. Let me see . . .'

Through my tears, I inspect the file, the pieces of

paper, hold them up to the light, sniff them. If only I can work it out . . . I *have* to work it out . . .

'Agatha, no. This isn't a test, child.' The professor takes my hands and removes the paper from them. 'Not a test,' she says again.

I meet her gaze, but her eyes show a panic which I've never seen before. Professor D'Oliveira, of all people, has always appeared unflappable.

My anxiety levels rise further. 'So, if this isn't part of the Trial, what is it?'

The professor looks around the room, as though searching for inspiration. 'I honestly don't know . . . Somebody has removed them.'

'That's impossible,' Sofia says. 'Nobody could have gained access to them without the highest clearance.' She doesn't appear even slightly surprised, I notice. Her manner has been calm and cold this whole time. Perhaps she doesn't feel emotion. I wonder if she's an advanced type of robot.

'And yet they are gone,' the professor replies brusquely, shooting her a fierce look that suggests she is challenging her to argue the point.

'But you must have a copy?' I say. My legs are wobbly and I feel like I'm going to faint. I sit down on a chair beside the cabinet.

The professor shakes her head. 'We don't keep copies of these records; they're classified. That's why they're under such high security. I do, of course, know some of the detail from the files; I even have a few notes of my own, some cuttings at home . . .'

'Who could have taken them?' I say. 'The security in this room is like the Bank of England.'

'You are right, Agatha. Nobody from outside the Guild could have made it in here to steal or destroy the files, without someone noticing. This room is guarded twenty-four-seven, all year round. The cabinet is fitted with a complex mechanical lock, which would shut down completely and sound an alarm if someone without the correct key attempted to gain access.'

There is a strange tone in her voice.

'Then, if it's not someone from the outside, what are you saying?' I ask – though the answer's obvious.

'What I'm saying, child, is that there must be a mole in the Guild.'

8.

HOMEWORK

There is a moment's silence, while the three of us digest this information.

My brain is behaving badly – it's slow and sluggish. It feels like there's a stone in my belly, heavy and cold.

'A mole?' I say at last. 'You mean – a Guild member has stolen my mother's file?'

The professor is rubbing her forehead as if she has a headache. 'That is the only logical explanation. Though how . . . or why . . .' She turns to Sofia. 'It's very late, and both you and our new recruit need to get some rest. Please take Agatha to the induction room, and give her a copy of the handbook to take home. You may then escort her out of headquarters, and go home yourself. If there is a mole in the organisation, our security could be compromised. I have to look into this straight away.'

'But don't you need my help?' says Sofia.

The professor sighs. 'I need you to follow my orders, Ms Solokov.'

'Of course, Professor D'Oliveira,' says Sofia, in an obedient tone. Even in my confounded state, I can't help noticing the look of anger that flashes in her eyes.

The professor marches over to the archive assistants' desk, and I can see her pointing at the blank pages in the file as she starts to explain the situation to the young assistant. A tiny part of me is hoping the girl will magically draw the real file out from behind the desk, where she's been keeping it safe. But her face goes from smiley to bewildered. She keeps shaking her head, clearly denying all knowledge of what could have happened – denying, no doubt, even the possibility of a file in this esteemed, ultra-secure file room being tampered with at all.

Soon, all the archive assistants are gathered round, deep in discussion with Professor D'Oliveira. I would like to stay and observe, but Sofia is dragging me along by the sleeve of my sweater. My legs are still wobbly and they're slow to respond, as if they're being controlled by an incompetent puppeteer.

'Come on,' she says, impatiently.

I bumble along behind her towards the exit. We have to stand still to be searched on the way out.

By the time I make it out of the archive room, Sofia is standing in the corridor, harrumphing loudly. 'What is it with you?' she says. 'They're all making such a fuss – like you're some kind of prodigal daughter or something. But as far as I can see, you're just some geeky kid who's struck lucky with a couple of Guild tests.'

I pull myself together quickly. 'The Guild Trial,' I correct her. I don't want Sofia to see me looking upset, so I start to think positively. Surely Mum's file has just been mislaid, and the professor will soon hunt it down? I feel better immediately.

Sofia rolls her eyes. 'You're just a little kid who needs a babysitter.'

'I really don't,' I tell her. I manage not to add *especially not you*. I pause, wondering whether to carry on and confront her. At last I say, 'What do you know about my mother's file?' I watch her face carefully for micro-expressions – the almost indiscernible twitches and tics that give away emotion – searching for signs of guilt. But there's nothing. If she *is* guilty, she's learnt amazing self-control.

She stares at me. 'What do you mean? I've never even seen the file.'

'How do I know that's true? Maybe you weren't too pleased about having your "youngest ever" record stolen by a new girl? Maybe you came here earlier, to remove the file, so you could make me feel as angry and hurt as you were feeling.'

Sofia flushes, but it appears to be with anger, rather than guilt. She advances towards me, and I'm suddenly very aware of the fact that she is considerably taller than me. I close my eyes for a moment and try to recall some of the self-defence moves Mr Zhang has taught me, but I can only summon up one of the most basic 'forms', which at best might be good for amusing her.

'Why are your eyes closed?' She sounds taken aback.

I open my eyes at once. 'I was trying to remember some self-defence,' I admit.

She laughs loudly. 'You don't really think I'm going to hurt you, do you?' She moves her face right down to mine. 'You are like a little bug – I don't care enough about you to squash you.'

'Thank you,' I croak. *Thank you?* What am I thinking? Am I really thanking her for not squashing me?

'I want to keep my position here,' she tells me. 'I am not going to risk it for the sake of stealing files about some kid's mum.'

I take a breath. 'Well, now we've cleared that up, what is it you're supposed to show me?'

She snorts. 'Come on.' She marches down corridor after corridor, and I have to run to keep up. I start to wish I had some of those trainers with wheels that little kids have – heelies.

Finally, she stops at a door and uses her Guild key to gain access. I'm pretty sure we're close to the Serpentine cavern, and I'm certain the professor's office is close by, even though I've only visited it once, when Liam and I were caught exploring the tunnels. By the time I catch up, Sofia is tutting and sighing like a displeased schoolmistress. I come close to pointing out to her that she is still only a teenager herself.

We step from plush carpeting on to wooden flooring, and she waits while the heavy door swings shut behind us; she doesn't use her key to lock the door. I've noticed the Guild doors tend to be self-locking. Our footsteps echo as we walk along the corridor, past glass cubicles, all of which are empty. Each one bears a number on its door, plus the name of a different staff member.

'Why is there no one here?' I ask as I jog along behind her.

She checks her watch. 'Because it's gone midnight.' She says this as if it's obvious.

'But . . . aren't there people on duty all the time? The file rooms were full of workers.'

'The administrative staff are different – they work shifts. Apart from them, there are agents and support staff on call all the time – they can be contacted wherever they are, in case of an urgent situation. But most people who work for the Guild have other jobs too – and sleep is important, to maintain full brain function.'

She definitely talks a little like a robot. She stops in front of a door that looks like all the others, except that it's number 563 (563? How big is this place?) and bears the words INDUCTION ROOM.

'Here's your jail cell.' She opens the door and steps aside for me to enter first. For a moment, I think she really is about to shut the door on me and walk away. My face must betray my concern, because she laughs a little nastily and says, 'Much as I'd love to leave you locked in here, I have a job to do.'

I step inside and scan the room. It's bigger than the other offices we've passed. There are around twenty small round tables set quite far apart from one another, each with its own blue upholstered chair. She points to a chair at one of the tables.

'You might as well sit here for a minute.'

I set down my backpack and take a seat. The chair is so comfortable I have to fight the urge to take a nap. I haven't slept all night, and I've run round London and walked for miles – or what feels like it. Instead, I continue to look around me. There are floor-to-ceiling bookcases lining the room. Most of the books are modern and their arrangement appears haphazard, with tall hardbacks alongside skinny paperbacks. There's one of those ladders that you can slide from left to right, for you to reach the higher shelves. It's like a more practical, less glamorous version of the library in Brianna's house, minus the reading balcony. Sofia walks over to a shelf and draws out a huge tome – it takes her both hands to carry it, and even then she grunts with the effort of carrying it over. She dumps it unceremoniously on the table in front of me.

'Take this home with you and start on page one,' she says.

I stare at the thick volume and read its long title.

A CONCISE HANDBOOK

of the

Rules, Regulations and Guidelines

Governing Conduct

for

MEMBERS OF THE

GATEKEEPERS' GUILD

'How many pages are there?'

'Three thousand and fifty-one.'

'Am I meant to read them all?' I ask in a small voice.

'If you want to become a fully fledged agent, yes, you are.'

I try not to show how disheartened I am by the task ahead of me. Normally, I love reading, but this . . . I flick to the back and see the heading *Rule Number 2,041.*

I look up at her. 'I don't have time to read this now. You see . . . I have to find out what happened to my mum.'

'You need to leave this one to the big dogs, little pup. Professor D'Oliveira is on the case.'

Little pup? Yuck! I decide to try a different tack. 'Actually, I'm already investigating a case at the moment.'

Sofia raises an eyebrow. 'Are you indeed?'

'Yes, it's to do with that murder at the British Museum. I think it's linked to the sinkhole in Bernie Spain Gardens – you know, the one that swallowed the ice-cream van.'

She crosses her arms and perches on the table in front of me. 'What makes you think there's a link?'

'Well . . . it's more of a hunch than anything, if I'm honest. But someone warned me off investigating the sinkhole . . .'

She sits forward. 'Who did?'

'I'm not sure. They were heavily disguised.'

'I see. So a person in a costume told you not to inspect a sinkhole, and that means you have to investigate a murder?'

'I know it sounds irrational! But how would they know I'd be visiting the sinkhole, unless they'd been watching me for some time, while I was looking into the museum case? So that means the two things are almost certainly connected. They don't want me to find out how the events are linked – that's why they told me to stop.'

She starts laughing. Worse, she removes my beret and ruffles my hair, as if I'm an entertaining toddler. 'You have a wild imagination, little girl.'

'I'm not a little girl. I'm a Guild agent, just like you.'

She raises an eyebrow. 'You think you're just like me, huh? Do you know how old I was when I left my parents to become a Gatekeeper?'

I shake my head.

'Nine. I was offered the chance to train as an undercover child agent, and I jumped at it. You think you know anything about real life, at your exclusive school for privileged brats?'

How did we get here? 'You think I'm a "privileged brat"? I'm there on a scholarship! But this is about me not abandoning a case in progress!'

'I see. And you think the Guild should support you in this?' She doesn't even try to keep the sneer out of her voice.

'Not support me – but just let me finish my investigation.' She snorts and her ponytail flies up like a mane. I suddenly realise that she's not so much of a robot as a horse – one of those purebreds that are hard to tame.

'Look, Oddball – or whatever your name is – you are just a cadet, OK? You don't get to come in here and start choosing your own investigations. Just because your mum was some sweetheart of the whole organisation, it doesn't give you special status. If you don't toe the line, you'll have your Guild key confiscated and be kicked out. Then you'll just be an ordinary kid again.' She says this with a mean grin, as if she can think of nothing better.

I look at her, wide-eyed. 'I don't want special status. It's just this is really important – I think something major is afoot.'

She stands up. 'Like I said, you're just a cadet. Now, take home the nice storybook and read it like a good little girl.' She rummages in her bag – a large black briefcase – and brings out a folder. 'And here's your homework.'

'Homework?'

'Puzzles, codes – that kind of thing.'

She hands me the folder and I shove it into my backpack. I try to squeeze the handbook in as well, but it won't fit. Seeing me struggle, she picks it up for me.

'I will carry it for you, for now,' she says. This is the first bit of kindness she's shown me.

'Thank you,' I say meekly.

I drag myself to standing and trail after her all the way back down the corridor, towards the entrance. Just before we reach the front door, she turns off to the left.

'Come on.'

My legs are so heavy with exhaustion, I could sink to the floor and weep. 'I thought we were going home.'

'I've just seen a light on. There's someone you should meet.'

Can't it wait till another day? I wonder. But she's already striding ahead. I see her stop in front of a door and knock before opening it.

I catch her up. On the open door, I read the name WALLACE JONES, QUARTERMASTER.

'Here she is,' says Sofia.

I join her in the doorway. Inside, seated at a wide desk, is a man who seems to take up a lot of room. His office is one of the larger cubicles, but he reminds me of Alice, when she encounters the EAT ME cake and does indeed eat it. (As if everyone doesn't know you should never eat anything if you don't know where it's come from!) Not that Mr Jones fills his entire room or anything – it's just that everything about him seems squeezed in: his clothes look too tight; his chair and desk too small; even his skin looks stretched. I get the feeling that, if he stood up, his head would touch the ceiling.

'Clara's daughter – we meet at last!' he says, coming out from behind his desk to clasp my hand. He has a friendly, open manner, and his hand is warm and dry.

'I'll leave you then,' says Sofia. She places the tome on the corner of Mr Jones's desk. I have no idea how I'll transport it home.

'Thank you, Ms Solokov,' he says, smiling at her, and she nearly smiles back – the corners of her lips twitch. Amazing – even Sofia appears less surly in his company.

'Come in, come in,' he tells me, drawing up a comfy-looking armchair, and gesturing for me to sit in it. I put my backpack down and sink on to the cushioned seat.

'Hard day?' he asks, going back to his own chair.

I nod. 'I only just passed the Trial, and then we got to the file rooms, and . . .' I tail off. It occurs to me that I don't yet know if the missing file is classified information.

Wallace Jones doesn't push me, though. He smiles and nods. 'Too much at once?' Then his face is suddenly filled with sorrow. 'So very sad about your mother. We all cherished her here, you know. She was one of our best.'

'Can I . . .?' I hesitate, not sure how to ask such a big, important thing of someone I've just met.

'What?' he prompts.

'Do you know what happened to her?'

He sits back with a thoughtful expression. 'I heard there was a nasty accident with that bike of hers. She always loaded it up with books. I used to beg her to leave some of them behind.'

I shake my head. 'It wasn't the bike.'

He frowns. 'It wasn't?'

'The bike is intact – not a scratch on it.'

He leans forward. 'Really? That is suspicious then. I had no idea. When did you see it? I assumed the police had confiscated it, after the accident.'

I hesitate. 'Well, I haven't seen it for a while. It's gone missing.'

'The police must have it,' he says.

'Maybe they came back for it . . . I haven't had a chance to ask Professor D'Oliveira.'

'Anyway, we are overlooking one very important fact, my dear.'

I hold my breath. Mr Jones is about to tell me something about my mum – something vital, that will help unlock all the answers.

'You are now a Gatekeeper! That must be celebrated!'

The breath leaves me like air bursting from a punctured tyre.

'There will be a lot of people watching you, as the daughter of Clara Oddlow,' he continues, wagging a finger at me – but he is smiling again. He lowers his voice to a whisper and leans towards me across the desk. 'Don't let them intimidate you, Agatha. You go at your own pace, and I'm sure you will do great things.'

'Thank you.'

'I've already heard that you are quite the talented young lady.' He beams again. Then he looks around his office. 'So . . . do you know what I do?'

'You're the quartermaster. I think, in the military, they are in charge of provisions and stuff?'

'Exactly. I am in charge of stuff!'

I can feel my face get hot. 'I mean . . .'

'Don't get flustered, my dear. It's a good description for the wide variety of . . . *stuff* I have to buy in. Imagine having to order thousands of rolls of loo paper, and then have them brought in to a secret underground base without arousing attention . . .'

I hadn't thought about that. 'How do you do it?'

He taps the side of his nose. 'Ahhh, need-to-know basis, I'm afraid.'

Although I'm fascinated by Mr Jones and his demanding job, my fatigue takes over and I can't stifle a yawn.

'My dear child, you are exhausted,' he says. 'Go home, go home!' He stands up and holds out a small paper bag with things in it. 'Consider it a welcome present, if you will.'

I thank him and get to my feet, reaching for the massive handbook.

'Leave it, leave it!' he says.

'But the professor . . .'

He holds up a hand. 'I will explain that it's far too heavy for you to take home, and I'm sure the professor will understand. I will have it returned to the induction room, for your next visit.'

With that, he helps me to put on my backpack then escorts me out of this section, into the main corridor. I'm starting to get a feel for the geography of the Guild's network now: there is one main tunnel, off which all the others branch, but I'm grateful that Mr Jones is making sure I'm heading in the right direction. He gives my shoulder a friendly squeeze and, as I walk away, I realise that I feel lighter, as if Wallace Jones not only buys in solid things, like toilet rolls, but also obtains and distributes necessities you can't touch, such as kindness and goodwill. Even the thought of my mum's file having disappeared doesn't seem quite so bleak now. After all, the professor is on the case.

I stop for a moment in the tunnel to examine the contents of the paper bag. There are two items: a transparent pen that glows in my hand with a weird light; and a small pager – a square electronic keypad, that allows you to send and receive messages. There's a note in the bag: *Page 6662 if ever you find yourself in danger.* I slip the two gifts back inside the paper bag, put it inside my backpack and continue on my way.

I can barely stand, let alone walk, but somehow I stumble on and find my way to the staircase that leads up to the top of Wellington Arch in Hyde Park.

I don't take this staircase in daytime as there's a viewing gallery up here, and tourists might get quite a shock at my sudden materialisation. But at this time of night no one is likely to spot a girl appearing as if by magic from behind the statue of the Angel of Peace.

I drag myself across the park, back to the cottage, and let myself in through the front door, confident that Dad will be asleep. I glance at my bedside clock as I throw myself on to my bed. Quarter past two – thank goodness it's Friday night, so I don't have school in a few hours. I say 'Goodnight, Mum,' to her photo, and fall asleep.

9.

SMUGGLERS' DOCK

I wake up late, feeling depressed, and for a moment I can't remember why.

Then I'm hit hard by the memory of what happened the day before. The file I'd waited so long to read, wiped completely blank. The cold stone is back in my belly, and it feels a little like losing Mum all over again.

In one sense, I've got what I wanted. But in another way, I've failed. I may have passed the Trial, but I haven't got one of the main things I took the Trial for. It's like learning to drive a car on the day that all the petrol runs out. I'm still no closer to finding out what happened to Mum. I look around the room despondently at the strewn clothes, many of them parts of my disguises. I look at my map of London on the wall, dotted with coloured pins and pieces of string. I look at the shelf full of notebooks – with black covers for general cases, and red for details of Mum's life and habits. It all feels rather silly, rather pointless.

What am I investigating for anyway? What makes me think I'm a detective? Why do I even want to be a detective? If it's to find out what happened to Mum, I've categorically failed, and, anyway, it doesn't seem like a particularly good reason to have chosen this career. Also, if we move to Cornwall for Dad's work, I won't be able to keep visiting Guild headquarters and complete my training with Sofia the robot-horse.

After a long time in bed, staring up out of the skylight at the blue September sky, I force myself to get up. I slip on my tartan slippers (granddad-style, but I like them) and pad downstairs to the kitchen. It looks like Dad has already been up, had his breakfast, and left. He doesn't work every Saturday, but sometimes he gardens even if he's not on the rota – he can't keep away from plants.

To cheer myself up, I take the time to make myself a luxury hot chocolate. The smell is blissful. For extra decadence, I grab a canister of squirty cream from the fridge and spray a large dollop on top. I sit at the kitchen table, cradling the warm mug and staring through the doorway at the photos that hang in the hallway. A lot of them are of me when I was younger, and there are several of Mum.

There she is, holding on to my arms as a toddler as I wade into the sea wearing a frilly pink bathing suit and gigantic inflatable armbands. There she is, hovering in the background as I blow the candles out on my seventh birthday cake, which she and Dad baked and iced together – a pirate ship, complete with sails and masts, which was what I'd asked for that year. And there she is again, just a few months before her accident, standing with me and Dad on Waterloo Bridge.

I remember how we had asked a tourist to take the picture for us. We're all smiling, and Mum's head is cocked to one side, so that it rests gently on top of my own.

I sip at the hot drink and, with each sugary gulp, a little more of the fog seems to clear from my brain. Mornings are always the worst time for doubting yourself, I think. I wonder if everybody is like this, all the great musicians and poets and painters, when they think about their life's work first thing in the morning. Do they all doubt themselves as much as I do? By the time I reach the bottom of the mug of hot chocolate, I feel more like myself.

I can't give up now. I have to find out what happened to Mum; I will still do what I can to avenge her. But that will have to wait until the professor has finished her own investigation into the missing file. In the meantime, I need to do something to keep the grey cells busy while I'm waiting. Otherwise, I'll just obsess about the situation.

I decide to ignore Sofia's warning and continue with my British Museum case. I'm sure Mum wouldn't have been deterred by anyone else's advice, so why should I let it stop me?

I rinse out the mug in the sink and run back up to my room, where I quickly get dressed. I opt for denim cut-off shorts with a sleeveless black turtleneck top. Staring at me unpleasantly from my desk, where I left it the night before, sits the homework set by Sofia in its bulging folder. I can't even bear to look at it. The thought of doing any more codes, breaking any more puzzles, just to gain her approval, seems ridiculous now.

Sofia thinks I know nothing about the real world, but surely I know more than a girl who sacrificed her childhood to a secret agency? I will not be distracted from my mission any longer. I pull on socks and my biggest, clumpiest pair of boots – the Doc Martens – and get out my mobile phone. While it's turning on, I go downstairs and quickly brush my teeth. When I call Liam, he does not pick up.

I try Brianna's number instead, and she answers after the second ring.

'Yo, how's it going?'

'Not bad. Any idea why Liam isn't answering his phone?'

'It's Saturday. He has tennis practice with that coach his guardian hired.'

I strike my forehead with my palm. 'Oh, right,' I say. 'I completely forgot!'

'What was it you wanted to talk about?' she asks.

'Well, I'm on a case. I was wondering . . . would you like to come down to the tunnels with me?'

'You mean, because your first choice isn't available?'

I feel myself flush. 'No, I was going to invite both of you . . .'

She laughs. 'Relax! I'm just teasing you. I'd love to come! What do I need to bring?'

Brianna knows about the tunnels, but she's never been down there. I've described them to her in general terms, as tunnels left over from former times – from the Tube and sewer networks, and the remains of Cold War bunkers – but I've never told her they're governed by a top-secret organisation called the Gatekeepers' Guild, and I've always discouraged her from investigating the tunnels herself. I've been careful to protect the Guild's secrecy, even from one of my best friends. But the Gatekeepers have failed me – I trusted them to keep my mother's secrets safe, and they let me down. Why should I protect their secrets now?

We chat for a few minutes more, and I think out loud over the phone about items she could bring to help us. By the time I hang up, I've listed one or two gadgets that Brianna has in her high-tech crime room, and I've suggested she bring her tool bag with maybe a screwdriver and file for tampering with locks, and we've agreed to meet up at a café opposite the British Museum.

I go on foot to meet her. It takes a good half-hour at a fast walk, but I don't have much pocket money left for a bus or Tube. Also, the weather is still fine, and I could do with the fresh air if we're going back underground. I start to regret this decision almost immediately, when I have to navigate a group of tourists having their pictures taken beside Marble Arch. By the time I arrive at Oxford Street, the crowds are heaving. I quickly turn off and take backstreets the rest of the way to the café opposite the museum.

Brianna is already sitting at a table when I enter. I don't recognise her at first, until she waves to me.

'What happened to your hair?' Her blue hair has been dyed back to a sedate brown.

She shrugs. 'Got to do as I'm told, or Doc Hargrave might suspend me. The seniors will stop my allowance if that happens.'

It's a shame. I liked the blue hair, which suited her personality. She smiles ruefully.

'Do I look very dull?'

In her ripped jeans, with her leather biker jacket, multiple earrings and half-shaved hair, I don't think Brianna could ever be described as 'dull'.

'Definitely not,' I reassure her.

'So, do you want something to drink, or shall we get going?'

'Let's just go.'

She swigs the last of her tea, and grabs her bag. It's a big duffel bag, which looks like something a soldier might carry. As we step out of the café, she salutes me smartly and says, 'So, where first, ma'am?'

'Did you bring the seismograph?'

She pats the duffel bag. 'Of course.'

'Let's set that up first, somewhere near the museum – I want to record any tremors.'

'I've got an app on my phone – so I'll get data directly if anything happens.'

She sets up the seismograph on one of the lawned areas in the courtyard of the museum. The machine is solar-powered and looks like a small yellow case. She places it with the lid open. Inside the lid, there's a screen which tracks movements under the ground. Usually, seismographs are used to monitor earthquakes, but I want to find out if anyone is doing too much drilling and excavating – enough to cause sinkholes like the one in Bernie Spain Gardens, for instance.

'Remind me why you own this thing,' I say.

She shrugs. 'They were selling them online and it looked cool.'

'Too much money,' I say, shaking my head.

'Hey! You're benefiting, so I wouldn't start complaining.'

'Good point.'

One or two people shoot us curious glances as we position the seismograph, and Brianna checks it's communicating with the app on her phone. No one tries to stop us, though. Hopefully, we look like we're just doing some kind of school project. Brianna unrolls a length of striped warning tape and places it round the machine, to keep people away.

'Right,' I say quietly, 'ready to go underground?'

'Try and stop me.'

It doesn't take long for me to spot a grille behind a large fir tree. We squeeze past the scratchy branches, until we're crouching in front of it.

'It looks like it takes one of those big old-fashioned keys,' says Brianna, pointing to the lock.

'Like this?' I hold out my key on its silver chain.

'Seriously – you carry a massive key around with you?'

'You have a lot of catching up to do. But, yeah, this key opens secret gates, doors and gratings all over London.'

'Cool,' she breathes. 'Where did you get it?'

'I'll tell you later.' I fit my key in the lock. It opens

with the same perfectly oiled motion as most of the other locks. The Gatekeepers certainly know how to maintain their property.

Together, we swing the grille up and I nod for her to go first down the stone steps. She does, and I follow, closing the grille and checking it locks behind us.

'Creepy,' she says. Then a light comes on. I can't work out where it's coming from.

'What is that?' I ask, following her down the stairs.

'Just the torch on my mobile.'

'OK . . .' I curse myself for not having remembered mobiles have torches: that would have been useful the last time I found myself in the dark.

'How long do these stairs go on for?' she asks.

'I've no idea – but not much longer, I'm guessing. We should arrive in a tunnel in a moment or two.'

Her next words suggest she's reached the bottom: 'Wow! Agatha, get down here.'

I arrive just after her. The tunnel is a standard Guild tunnel: well maintained in terms of cleanliness, but otherwise nothing special. The walls are mainly concrete, but there are patches of stone and brickwork –

presumably areas that have been filled in and repaired over the decades.

'Where are we?' she asks.

I point to a passage that branches off to the right. 'If my sense of direction is correct, we should get to the British Museum Tube station if we head that way.' I want to take another look at the station, to see if it's still being used and if there are any new clues.

'The British Museum doesn't have a Tube.'

'Didn't we tell you about the station? It used to be part of the Central line.'

She stares, wide-eyed. 'There's an abandoned stop down here?'

'Well, there's actually more than one. But this is the one we're interested in.'

'I'm interested in all of them.'

'OK, rail geek – maybe another time.'

She nods eagerly. Her face is eerie in the half-light of the dark tunnel, picked out only by the light from her phone.

I shiver. 'Come on – let's get moving.'

It takes less than five minutes to find the rail track and another ten to reach the door that gives access to the museum station under the street called High Holborn. Just as we reach the door, we hear a train pass close by; it creates a gust of wind that hits us with surprising force, and Brianna looks nervous.

'Are you sure the trains don't run along here any more?'

'Not along this bit, no.'

I fish out my key and unlock the door. Once through to the station, Brianna lets out a low whistle.

'Look at this place! It's like a museum in its own right.' She points to the Ovaltine advertisement. 'Look how old the posters are!'

I smile. 'I promised you amazing, didn't I?'

She walks a few steps further and stops in front of a huge roll of metal. It's one of several standing along the wall at the side of the platform, together with some large canisters. 'What's this?'

I join her, frowning. The metal is silver-coloured and flat, rather than rounded like wire. I've seen it before, in the chemistry lab at school. 'It looks like magnesium ribbon.' The canisters beside the metal rolls bear the words IRON OXIDE or ALUMINIUM POWDER.

'None of this was here the last time I was down here,' I say. My brain is computing. *Iron oxide, aluminium powder and magnesium ribbon equal . . . Iron oxide, aluminium powder and magnesium ribbon equal . . . Come on, brain!*

'What do you think it's for?' Brianna asks.

I Change Channel and watch the ingredients come to life. The magnesium ribbon uncoils and sets itself alight. It then approaches the iron oxide and aluminium powder and the whole thing goes . . . *CABOOM!*

'Thermite!' I shout, relieved I got there. Brianna jumps. 'Sorry,' I say, 'I was just working it out.'

'Thermite? What's that?'

'A mixture that causes an intensely hot chemical reaction that can melt through steel.'

We stare at each other for a moment.

'Why . . .?' she begins.

'I'm not sure. And there's so much of it . . .'

'Do you think that's what caused the sinkhole?' she asks.

I nod. 'Quite possibly. If someone's blasting out large sections of tunnel, that could easily cause a cave-in like the one I saw.'

We spend a few minutes in the station. Brianna mainly explores – exclaiming at other old posters and features like old telephones – but I look for fresh footprints and check there aren't other chemicals or weapons being stored. I find nothing else suspicious.

'You ready to go?' I ask Brianna. 'I'm thinking whoever caused that sinkhole must have other plans for the rest of the explosives. There's enough there to take down the Tower of London. They're not going to be too happy, if they catch us in here with their stash.'

She rolls her eyes. 'Life's never dull with you, Agatha Oddlow. How do you always stumble on the dangerous stuff?'

I grin. 'Would you rather I went back to investigating the school teachers?'

'Er . . . no! This is way more fun.' She grins back. 'Now, let's get out of here.'

As we head out of the station and back into the tunnels, I muse on our find.

'What do you think they're going to do with all that thermite?'

'Maybe they *are* going to blow up the Tower of London,' she suggests.

'But they wouldn't store it at the British Museum station, in that case. It's too far away.'

Brianna stops to think. 'More mining, perhaps?'

'What for, though? Where are they trying to get to?'

'I don't know.' Brianna shrugs. 'Shall we go and explore underneath that sinkhole – see if there are any answers there?'

'Exactly what I was about to suggest,' I say.

As we walk, I begin to tell her about the Gatekeepers' Guild, and about the lies surrounding Mum's death. My head feels like it's going to explode if I don't talk to someone. I do feel some pangs of guilt at betraying their secrets – but I trust Brianna not to blurt it all out to anyone. I've already admitted to myself that my obsession with this investigation is partly to distract me from focusing on Mum's missing bike and that empty file, both of which are niggling away the whole time in the back of my mind. Has the professor made any progress in working out who took the records from the file? I wish I knew.

'So, the whole folder was empty?' she says, in horror, when I get to the end of my story.

'Yep. Just blank sheets of paper.'

'You must've felt . . .' She doesn't finish the sentence.

'Yeah,' I confirm. 'And there must be a mole – because whoever—'

I don't finish the sentence because she takes me by surprise, throwing her arms round me in a big hug. For a moment, my whole body stiffens at the unexpected physical contact, but then I respond by hugging her back. She holds me for a long time, and it takes me a while to realise I'm crying.

'Sorry,' I say, wiping my eyes in embarrassment when we let each other go.

'No, it's fine. I can't imagine how hard it's been on you. So you really thought these Guild people were going to tell you what happened to your mum?'

I pause. 'I don't know . . . I mean, I think, if they actually knew, they'd already have told me . . . but I'm sure they suspect something or someone – and I thought the file would give me useful information – you know, who she was working with, who she was investigating; or if she had any enemies, that kind of thing.'

'We'll find out,' she says. She sounds so determined that I almost believe we can do it.

We start to walk again, heading towards the South Bank.

A train passes close by and we instinctively shrink against the wall, laughing when we realise it's in a separate tunnel.

'That must be the Waterloo and City line,' I say, after the near-deafening shuddering dies down.

'Is that the one that shuttles between Waterloo and Bank?'

'That's right – the shortest Tube line in London.'

'And what's that?' asks Brianna, pointing a little way ahead. 'It looks different from the other tunnels.'

It's a passageway that shouldn't be there, according to my inner map. The work looks amateur: irregular, as if it was done in a hurry.

'This must be the blast that caused the sinkhole,' I say. 'I don't think this is Guild work. Their tunnels are much better constructed.'

We walk cautiously towards the opening, taking care not to stumble over the uneven ground.

'What use would a tunnel be at this point?' I wonder aloud.

'Maybe there's something they needed access to?' she suggests.

'So they had to blast a tunnel to get there . . . It makes sense. Shall we see where it leads? It might give us some answers.'

She shines her phone's torch along the tunnel. It's filled with rubble.

'Are we under Bernie Spain Gardens?' she asks.

I close my eyes and conjure up my map of the

Embankment and South Bank area. I picture the River Thames and the Oxo Tower, and the rectangle of grass that marks Bernie Spain Gardens.

'Yeah, I reckon so. So they made their tunnel and caused a cave-in, but didn't bother to clear it up.'

'Maybe they didn't have time,' she says.

I nod to her duffel bag. 'Have you got a bulldozer or excavator in that kit?'

'Yeah, plus hard hats and three workmen.' We both laugh, but stop abruptly when we contemplate the task ahead.

We navigate our way through the debris, clambering over the larger boulders and trying not to stumble on the smaller lumps of concrete and stone. The air is dry and thick with dust. I try not to imagine what would happen if the roof here doesn't hold. Being buried alive doesn't sound like fun.

Brianna stops when we reach the sinkhole. The ice-cream van's been removed, leaving a gaping view of the cloudy sky. Steel props have been placed here and there, to prevent further collapse.

'It's kind of creepy,' she says, shivering.

I try to limit my breathing as we continue along the dusty passage. I remember how miners get a chronic lung disease called emphysema from inhaling coal dust. That is over long periods of time, of course, but still . . .

'Dusty,' says Brianna, holding a tissue over her face.

I nod, unwilling to talk and inhale more of the filth.

At the end of the passage, we arrive in a cavernous room – even larger than the cave beneath the Serpentine. There are signs of recent activity: cigarette stubs and a general lack of dust.

Brianna points to a steel door in one of the walls. 'Will your key open that, do you think?'

We walk over and read the signs plastered all around the area.

I pull out my key again. It fits and turns just as easily as in the other doors. So this is a Gatekeepers' development. Part of me was hoping the lock would resist – I don't want to accept that the Guild is responsible for the reckless use of explosives that caused the sinkhole.

We glance nervously at one another before pushing the door open.

'Do you have anything in that tool bag that could double as a weapon?' I whisper. She nods and sets her bag on the floor, rummaging through it until she draws out a hammer and a mallet. I take the hammer and we count to three before pushing the door open, brandishing our tools as if they'd be some use against guns . . . or grown-ups.

'What is this place?' says Brianna. We both stand still, letting the door shut behind us. 'Isn't that . . . water?'

We are in a giant subterranean room – far larger even than the cavern we just left. The ground runs out, and below us, dark and unwelcoming in the beam of Brianna's light, we can see water. We can hear it too: it's like a roar in the night, slamming against the rock.

'How far does it go? Is it an underground lake?' she says.

'It's an underground dock,' I say. 'I'm sure of it. We must be close to the Thames – I reckon the boats moor here and then take their cargo out to the river and on to their destination ports.'

'A . . . dock?' says Brianna. 'But who would use it?'

'Smugglers, I'm guessing.'

'Do you think other people know it's here?' she asks.

'It's not on any of the maps, so it must be a pretty well-kept secret. But don't forget the door opened with my Gatekeepers' key.'

She shines her light around as far as the beam will reach. 'I can't see any way for boats to get in – there seem to be walls all the way round.'

'Submarines?' I suggest. 'They could come through a submerged entrance.'

She lets out her trademark low whistle.

We're so engrossed in our big adventure that we forget to keep to the sides. When the overhead lights snap on, we're lit up like fish in a tank and it's too late to find a dark corner in which to hide. We stand, frozen, hammer and mallet held up, as if we're playing some oversize version of that Whac-A-Mole game.

Two men enter – large muscular men in dark suits. Brianna grabs my arm with one hand. I'm only vaguely aware that she's gripping it too tightly. My head is telling me to be prepared, to slow my breathing, to keep calm – to find my 'true balance', as Mr Zhang would say. But my body is telling me to run – to run as fast as I can, and not look back. I glance around in desperation, but I already know there's nowhere to go.

The men stop in surprise at the sight of us.

'Hey!' one of them shouts. 'What are you doing here?'

I run through responses in my head, but fail to come up with anything plausible.

Our dad dropped us off in his submarine, while he went for milk . . .

Did you see a mobile phone? I'm sure I dropped it in the Thames . . .

We're looking for the toilets . . .

The hammer feels slippery in my palms. I wipe them on my trousers, one at a time.

'I said, what are you doing here?' He's closer now – too close. I can smell his breath – high-tar cigarettes mixed with strong black coffee. His colleague stands behind him, an ominous shadow.

'I – I . . . we . . .' I stutter. My voice feels like it's full of lumps. They catch in my throat, and make it hard to speak. I glance at Brianna. She is pale and looks terrified. I draw breath. 'We're investigating,' I say at last.

'Investigating?' The man's spittle sprays my face, and I resist the urge to wipe it away. 'Who are you? Nancy Drew?'

'I don't know who that is,' I lie. I know full well she's a girl detective from old books, but I want to appear naive and innocent.

'We'd better take them in,' he says to his colleague, who nods.

The silent one strides over to Brianna and removes her mallet, just as Mr Spittle disarms me of my hammer. I run through possible scenarios in my head. None of the outcomes look good.

'Who do you work for?' I ask as he pins my arms behind my back. It hurts, but I manage not to cry out. I need to keep my cool if there's any chance of us coming out of this alive.

'You'll find out soon enough,' he says into my ear.

In a couple of seconds, they have us both restrained.

It's bad enough I've failed to protect myself at all – but I'm responsible for Brianna as well. She's letting out a tiny whimpering sound, like the whine of a mosquito. I close my eyes and picture my *sifu*. What would Mr Zhang have me do? I'm just too much of a beginner at martial arts for it to be of use. In a show of resistance, I manage to get my DM boot up and scrape the heel down my assailant's shin. He lets out a curse but doesn't relax his hold. I try going completely limp, but he seems prepared for this – he effortlessly throws me over his shoulder in one smooth movement.

Soon, Brianna and I are both being carried back along the tunnels like sacks of coal.

'Ow! You just knocked my head on the wall!' I complain, testing to see if he shows compassion. But this only gets me another hard knock – one I'm sure is deliberate.

'Where are you taking us?'

'You'll see.'

It's hard to breathe deeply while hanging over his shoulder but I can calm my thoughts, at least. After all, if they wanted to kill us, they could have thrown us in the water at the secret dock, and no one would ever have found out.

From my disadvantaged position, I try to get my bearings. I close my eyes and call up the maps I've seen of the tunnels. They appear in my mind's eye one at a time, and I dismiss them until I access the right one. But, wait a minute, this can't be right . . .

'Hey,' I hiss to Brianna. 'I think we're going to the Guild headquarters.'

'Really? That's good, right?'

I catch a glimpse of her face – it's still white and scared.

'Yeah,' I reassure her, 'it's good.'

The truth is, I'm not sure. Why would the Guild have a secret submarine dock under London? And who took Mum's bike, and who took her file? What if the Guild is full of traitors, and we've just walked straight into their net?

And why won't I ever learn caution, no matter how many times I'm caught?

10.

FOUND OUT

When we pass through the door to the offices I visited the night before, I twist my head and try to read the names on the doors along the way. We take the turning that leads past Wallace Jones's office, and I catch sight of him, large and placid, flicking through documents at his desk. I consider calling out to him, but we are gone before I've even fully summoned the thought.

Then we reach the door marked PROFESSOR D. D'OLIVEIRA. Brianna's guard knocks and we hear the professor's voice commanding us to enter.

They carry us in and drop us awkwardly into chairs. I knock my elbow and my tailbone – 'Ow!'

The professor nods to the men. 'Thank you. You may go.'

The guards nod and leave, shutting the door behind them. The room is as I remember it from my last visit, before the summer – complete with wood panelling, an enormous black and gold desk – and a rather stern Professor D'Oliveira sitting behind it in her green-leather chair.

'They were nice,' I say brightly as I rub my elbow. 'Really friendly. Great conversationalists.'

'Great people skills,' Brianna agrees. She looks shaken. I catch her eye and smile to reassure her.

There's an icy silence. The professor seems to be looking down at some paperwork. After a minute or two of Brianna and me pulling faces at each other and me mouthing, 'This is the professor I was telling you about,' (to much confused eyebrow-raising on Brianna's part), there is a knock on the door.

'Come!' says the professor. The door opens and I let out a groan – the new arrival is Sofia Solokov, my New Best Friend.

'Take a seat, Sofia,' says the professor. 'Thank you for joining us at such short notice.'

Sofia pulls up a chair and shoots me an evil look. 'Whatever she's been up to, it's got nothing to do with me,' she says, folding her arms.

The professor frowns. 'On the contrary, as long as you are her mentor, her antics have everything to do with you. An employee is only as good as his or her supervisor.'

I consider letting the professor continue – it makes a change to see Sofia getting it in the neck – but my fairness barometer kicks in. 'She didn't know,' I say.

The professor holds up a hand. 'That is enough. Now, you will both be quiet and listen to what I have to say. First of all, though, who is *this*?' She points to Brianna as if she is an ugly bluebottle that has flown in through a window and is buzzing around annoyingly.

My friend sits up very straight and waits until she's established eye contact with the professor, before saying, 'I'm Brianna Pike.'

'Are you indeed? And how did you come to stumble into my domain, I wonder?'

'Agatha brought me, because she's having an awful time about her mum,' says Brianna. I appreciate her loyalty, but now is not the time.

'Shut up!' I hiss, but Brianna is not about to stop:

'She's been waiting for years to find out the truth, but now the file's missing and she doesn't know if she'll ever know how her mum really died.'

There is a long silence.

The professor turns to me. 'Well, Miss Oddlow, you certainly lost no time in sharing our secrets with an outsider.'

I blush. *I'm sorry* would sound feeble, so I say nothing.

'You have only just qualified with us, yet you seem to hold little understanding of what it means to be a member of our organisation. Clearly, I have made a serious miscalculation in enlisting you.'

The room shrinks to my heartbeat. *Ba-boom! Ba-boom! Ba-boom!* 'Little understanding'? 'Serious miscalculation'?

'Professor, wait, please!' I beg. 'I had to carry on with my investigation, but Sofia said I wasn't allowed to choose my own case. I needed help – otherwise I would never have involved Brianna.'

'Ms Solokov was right. New recruits do not have the authority to choose their own investigations.'

Sofia smiles and shoots me a gloating look.

'Yes, but—'

'Those who cannot follow Guild orders,' says the professor, cutting me off, 'have no place within our structure.'

I stare at her. The cold stone in my belly has swollen to the size of a rock. 'But . . .'

She holds up her hand again. 'We have made the rules clear all along, child. There's no room for mavericks here. You, of all people, should understand why I need to know that every agent is fulfilling his or her duties, and not . . . branching off to further their own interests.'

My face grows hot.

'But . . .' I try again, 'there were the ingredients to make thermite – inside the abandoned British

Museum station! Someone has been using it for illegal activities.'

She shakes her head. 'You silly girl. Thermite is a well-known product for the welding of train tracks. That imagination of yours will get you into terrible trouble, if you don't rein it in. Not everything is a criminal plot!'

'But what about the Guild tunnel that collapsed, causing the sinkhole in Bernie Spain Gardens?'

She taps her fist on the desk, like a judge banging her gavel for order in court.

'Enough! You have been a Guild member for less than a day, yet you have already broken Guild protocol, trespassed in private areas, questioned my authority at every turn, and – what's worse – initiated a civilian into our secrets. These are breaches which cannot be tolerated. You will hand me your key at once.'

I shrink away from her and close my hand round the key. 'But it's mine.'

'That key is Guild property. You will kindly hand it over. Now.'

This can't be happening! My hand is shaking as it clutches at one of the last precious items left to me by Mum. 'No. It's mine. You can't take it – she left it to me.'

'Your mother was a fully trained Guild agent, and therefore entitled to the free movement which comes with the job. You have earned no such entitlement. Now, hand it over, or I will have to call one of the guards to take it by force.'

I have tears in my eyes as I unfasten the silver chain and wordlessly pass her the object that connected me most closely with my mum. What do I have now that was hers, apart from Oliver and some shelves of books?

'Ms Solokov, escort Miss Oddlow to Mr Jones's office, and explain that she's been suspended. Miss Pike and I need to have a little word. I will speak with you later about responsibilities.'

'Mum's bike is missing!' I blurt out in desperation. 'That can't be a coincidence – not with her file disappearing too.'

The professor surveys me coolly. 'Indeed? Then

that will also need to be looked into. Now, please do as I say and go with Ms Solokov.'

Sofia grabs my elbow and pulls me far too hard out of the room.

'Thank you, so very much,' she says in an angry whisper, delivered straight into my right ear. 'Things were going fantastically until you arrived and messed everything up. I told you not to go off on your own investigations. You think you know everything, don't you? Now I'm in it up to my ears, and you get to waltz off.'

I shake off her hold on my elbow and turn to face her.

'You think I want to waltz off?' I snap. 'I want to be part of this. I need to know what happened to my mum. And I also want to be an agent – more than almost anything.' A woman passing with a clipboard raises an eyebrow at the scene we're making, but she carries on walking. Sofia grabs my arm again and pulls me towards Wallace Jones's office.

Outside his door, I shake her off again and

straighten my clothes, smoothing my hair with my hands. She raps on his door.

'Come!'

Sofia steps inside, grabbing me and dragging me after her. 'Morning, Mr Jones. Professor D'Oliveira says Agatha Oddlow has to be suspended.'

He looks at me with evident curiosity. 'Already? It took your mother a full five weeks.'

'My mum was suspended?'

He smiles and gestures for me to take a seat. 'At least twice, if I remember rightly. She too was quite . . . impetuous.' He pauses for a moment, looking past me and Sofia, as if he is picturing Mum. 'Her instincts did tend to be correct, mind you.'

I feel a tiny splinter of hope and sit forward in my chair. 'So can you get me un-suspended?'

'No,' cuts in Sofia. 'The professor made it quite clear that—'

He holds up a hand. 'Thank you, Ms Solokov. I can take care of things from here.'

She looks furious, but nods and leaves, closing the door behind her (a little more forcefully than necessary).

He observes me in kindly silence for a moment. Then he leans towards me across his desk.

'Would you take some well-intended advice from an old hand?'

'Of course.'

'Don't be quite so . . . blatant about your contempt for the rules. When you're allowed back in to the fold, smile and nod and bow, and give the impression of having learnt your lesson. Can you do that?'

'I guess . . .'

He smiles. 'Good. You may go.'

I fish in my pocket for the pager and hold it out to him. 'Don't you want this back?'

'No, you can keep that. I'm sure you will be needing it very soon, if your exploits so far are anything to go by.'

'Thank you.' I get up. His phone rings and he gestures for me to wait.

The call is a short one, consisting merely of him saying, 'Right – I'll tell her.' He replaces the receiver.

'You're to meet your friend by the front door.'

'Thank you,' I say again. 'Not just for . . .' I'm

still close to tears, and I don't manage to complete the sentence.

'I know, my dear. My pleasure.'

I find Brianna by the front door – minus her bag of tools.

'Where's your bag?'

'Confiscated.'

'No! I'm sorry.'

She shrugs. 'Nothing irreplaceable.'

Unlike Mum's key.

The door opens, without either of us touching it.

'We'd better go,' I say. I point to a camera above our heads. 'I reckon they're watching, to make sure we leave.'

Brianna sticks her tongue out at the camera.

'Stop it!' I say. 'I'm still hoping to come back here, one day.'

'They deserve it. Patronising gits.'

I can't argue with her. Right now, I'm furious with the Guild, furious with Sofia Solokov, and extra furious with Professor D'Oliveira. They haven't listened to a word I've said and now there's no one investigating the massive quantity of thermite ingredients – nor the smugglers' cove. And they've taken my key . . . If I'm honest, though, I'm also angry with myself. I have messed up an amazing opportunity.

We walk in silence through the tunnels. We come up near Marble Arch, and I hug her quickly.

'Oh – are you going to the fireworks tomorrow night?' she asks. 'Liam and I are going, if you fancy it? Might be a nice diversion, after all this.'

I shake my head. 'I don't think I'd be very good company.'

She squeezes my arm. 'OK, I understand. Let us know if you change your mind.'

There's a small stab of pain somewhere in my chest, like a tiny pinprick. This is what I'll miss, if we move to Cornwall. How long would it take to get new friends like Brianna and Liam? I already know the answer – there are no friends quite like them.

I watch her as she heads off home to Cadogan Place. I don't feel like going back to Groundskeeper's

Cottage. After a moment's reflection, I realise I want to be near Mum.

I climb aboard a number 74 bus and watch London pass by as dejection sets in. I just got accepted as the youngest Gatekeeper ever – and now I'm nothing. It's worse than before I learnt about the Guild – because now I know what I'm missing out on. I've had a glimpse of a place where I could have fitted in – a place where having a talent for puzzles and code-breaking was actually considered a good thing.

I switch on my phone and discover I've had three texts from Liam.

R u free?

U out there?

HEY, AI WHY THE SILENT TREATMENT??

I text back.

Been suspended ☹

He texts back immediately.

On a Saturday???

I realise he thinks I mean suspended from school. I can sense his panic through the ether.

From Guild

Ohhhh ☹ What happened?

Don't want to talk about it at mo. Off to see Mum

You want company?

Nah. Thx though

Here if you need me

I put my phone away and once again contemplate my life to come if we move to Cornwall for Dad's job. No Brianna. No Liam. No London. No Gatekeepers' Guild. But I've already lost the Gatekeepers' Guild, haven't I? I think about what Wallace Jones said, about how Mum also got suspended. She obviously got reinstated. How did she do it? Could I be reinstated too?

The bus takes about half an hour to reach the gates of Brompton Cemetery. I wander along the familiar path to Mum's grave. When I get there, I wipe some moss from her stone. It's a horizontal stone, like a small bed. The book I left last time has gone. I hope someone's enjoying it. I sit down on her stone and begin to tell her about the past couple of days, including Dad's job offer.

'. . . So you see, I don't want to go, Mum. But it would be amazing for Dad – and I'm just being selfish, wanting to stay here. Anyway, now I've been suspended from the Guild . . .' I sigh. 'And it's tiring, having to worry about all this other stuff – you know, who's plotting what – instead of just making friends and getting my homework done.' I pause. I can't remember when I last did any homework. Great – another thing to get into trouble for.

I lie back on the stone. It's warm from the sun and I close my eyes. Mum becomes much clearer when I shut my eyes. I can picture her, in her tortoiseshell glasses and tweed skirt, which ought to make her look like she's never seen a mirror – but she carries it all off, so she looks quirky and interesting instead.

I can feel her stroking my hair, the way she used to, when she sat by my bed at night.

'It's OK, my love,' she tells me. 'You don't have to be responsible for everybody else. You can just give up, if that's what you want.' She is quiet for a moment or two, and then she says, 'But make sure it's what you want. I'm not sure my Agatha could ever be happy just being like everybody else.'

When I open my eyes, I can still feel her warmth for a few minutes. The stone in my belly has shrunk to a pebble, and I understand. Mum's given me her approval to give up detecting – at least for now – and just be me. But she's right: I will always need to find answers, in the same way as we all need oxygen to breathe.

I take the bus back to Marble Arch and walk across the park to the cottage. It's getting dark, but Dad is still out in the grounds and I run myself a bubble bath and lie back, with my copy of *Poirot Investigates*. The Belgian detective always makes me feel better.

I don't switch on my phone until I'm back in my room, pulling on my pyjamas. There's a text from Liam.

R u coming 2 fireworks 2moro?

I text back.

Not sure I feel up to it 😟

Might cheer you up? Take your mind off things?

Sorry – another time

I turn off my phone and lie on my bed, staring up through the skylight – where I once received a clue. Was it only two nights ago? Two nights ago, when I was still dreaming of being a Gatekeeper, of finding out what happened to Mum.

Dad comes home, but he seems distracted, and I don't feel much like talking either. We eat in front of the TV, and I retreat to my room to lie on my bed with my thoughts.

I fall asleep pondering what might have been if I'd remained a Gatekeeper, if Mum's file hadn't been stolen, if I hadn't blown everything.

11.

RUNNING OUT OF TIME

I'm feeling miserable when I wake up on Sunday morning. My clock says eight o'clock, so I've had more than thirteen hours' sleep. I switch on my phone. It beeps with a text from Brianna, but I'll read it later. I still don't feel in the mood to go to the fireworks. I sit up and slide my feet into my slippers.

'Meow!' Oliver stands up on my bedside chair. I hadn't even realised he was in here.

'Hey, boy. Shall we go down and see what we can rustle up to eat? Dead mouse? Or your favourite – mangled bird?'

When he was younger, Oliver was always catching

little birds and rodents, and bringing them home as gifts for Mum. She tried everything to discourage these gestures of love, but nothing worked. Nowadays, he's a more mature cat and less bloodthirsty. I can't say I miss his offerings.

I pull on my dressing gown, and we head down to the kitchen. I can see Dad through the window, in our private garden. He's weeding the borders and tying flowering plants to supports. When he's done that, he'll move on to pruning the hedges and mowing the lawn. Dad has trouble sitting still for any length of time.

After I've fed Oliver, while I'm stirring batter for pancakes, my phone beeps with another text. I lean over to check the screen: it's from Liam.

> Will miss u tonight at fireworks.
> U want me to come over instead?

I can't believe he'd be willing to miss the big display for me. I text back.

> No – you go and tell me about them. I want to live vicariously

His response comes immediately, making me laugh.

> What do vicars have to do with fireworks???

No one can make me laugh like Liam. I text back.

> It means to enjoy life through someone else's experiences

> Ahhh! K. Will take pix

> Thank you! ☺

I return to my breakfast preparations. I have two frying pans on the go at once, and soon I've used up all the batter and I have a stack of pancakes on a plate. I pour myself a glass of milk, grab the maple syrup and take it all through to the living room. Time for a binge of my latest favourite show on Netflix. It's the perfect antidote to my malaise – a drama series featuring an improbable chain of events, none of which can be explained rationally.

When the series ends, I move on to a show about zombies. Good thing Dad's still outside – I don't think he'd approve of my choices.

He appears around 2pm. He pokes his head in through the living-room doorway.

'What are you doing inside on such a lovely day?'

'Just a bit tired,' I tell him.

'You OK?'

'Fine.' I manage a smile. 'Just chilling with Oliver.'

'Well, make sure you get some air later, OK?'

'OK.'

I remain slumped on the sofa, with Oliver purring on my lap. I tell him who the different characters are, and explain why they're arguing or fighting. The cat is in ecstasy at all this company and attention. At least one of us is happy.

Around five o'clock, Dad comes back inside. I hear him stamping mud off his boots on the doorstep, and then the sound of the door shutting behind him. He shouts my name.

'Here!' I respond, but the living-room door is closed and I'm not sure if he hears.

I hear him filling the kettle and opening cupboards in the kitchen. At last, he appears in the living room doorway, carrying a mug of steaming tea and a packet of digestive biscuits. He stops at the sight of me, huddled under a throw, with the cat on top.

'Agatha – you haven't moved. What's wrong?'

I shrug. He comes to sit beside me on the sofa and pulls me in for a hug. He smells like earth with an undertone of sweat. It's strangely comforting – such a familiar Dad-odour.

'What's going on? Did you not hear the phone?'

'The phone?'

'The landline. I've just checked the voicemail. It's full of messages from Liam and Brianna, asking you to call them. Have you fallen out with them?'

I shake my head. 'They'll just be calling about the fireworks.'

'Of course. Aren't you going?' He studies me with

concern. 'I thought you were looking forward to the display.'

'I'm a bit tired today. Thought I'd give it a miss.'

'Is this all about Cornwall?'

I shake my head.

He stands for a moment, watching me. Then he says, 'Well, let them know you're all right, won't you? I don't want them turning up on the doorstep in a panic.'

'I'll let them know.'

'Is there anything I can get you?'

'No, thanks.'

'Brianna's voicemails all asked you to reply to her texts . . .?'

My mobile is in my dressing-gown pocket, and I extract it and turn it on. It beeps with a ridiculous number of notifications, some from Liam and others from Brianna.

I open the thread from Brianna:

Seismograph has picked up weird readings! Call me!

The next message just reads:

> ?????????????

She then resorts to:

> Earth calling Agatha: are you out there???

Her final text reads:

> Calling your landline. PICK UP!!

I should probably call her back, but the mention of the 'weird readings' has caused something to start clicking into place. I lift Oliver off my lap and set him gently down beside Dad on the sofa.

'Agatha – what's going on?'

Dad sounds concerned, but I just say, 'Got to work something out.'

I almost run through to the kitchen. My brain is whirring. I grab a pen and an envelope off the pile of unopened post (I must remind Dad to open some of the bills) and sit down at the table to make a list of possibly unconnected thoughts:

1. The Waterloo and City line runs every day except Sunday. Today is Sunday.
2. The Lord Mayor's Fireworks are also today.
3. The attendant at the British Museum might have been killed because he discovered the secret tunnel down to the abandoned Tube station.
4. The abandoned British Museum Tube station is linked by rail to the nearby Bank station, right by the Bank of England.
5. The British Museum station has a stash of highly explosive chemicals.
6. The Waterloo and City line starts near the Bank of England and ends south of the river, near the smugglers' dock that Brianna and I found.

I sit back as realisation dawns.

This is the link! Someone is planning a heist. They can use the thermite to blow through the vaults at the Bank of England, and then get away using the

Waterloo and City line and the underwater dock. The fireworks must be scheduled to disguise the sound of the explosions. And because it's a Sunday they can use the Waterloo and City line tunnels because no trains are running.

I run up to my room – there's no time to lose. I scroll quickly through Liam's texts, which are all about the fireworks. I send one text to both him and Brianna:

> Heist alert! Thermite for robbery @ Bank of E! Fireworks to divert attention & drown out explosion! Call police NOW! Am going in!

I survey my rails of clothes. I'm going to need to dress practically. I pull on dark-blue jeans and a navy hooded sweatshirt. I empty my backpack out on the bed. What do I need, what do I need? Then I stop for a minute, sitting with a thump down on the bed, as I have a heavy realisation: I haven't got my Guild key. I can't do anything to foil the plot if I can't get into the tunnels. Unless . . .

Last time, I gained entry to the museum through the tunnels. This time, I can do the opposite, and get down to the tunnels via the horrible hole behind the boiler. I check my watch. The British Museum closes at half five, and it's already twenty to six. I'm just going to have to go undercover. I grab a standard cleaner's tabard, in a fairly disgusting purply-brown colour (that's meant to be called 'puce', but which I can't help thinking of as 'puke'). I stuff it in my backpack, together with my name badge and head torch.

There's no sign of Dad, so I shout, 'Right, Dad, I'm off.'

He appears from the living room. 'Are you going to the fireworks?'

'Yep,' I say brightly. I don't add that I'll be experiencing them from below ground.

'Great. Enjoy yourself. Oh – here you go.'

He takes out his wallet and extracts a ten-pound note.

'Oh no – I'm fine for cash, thanks, Dad.' I feel bad enough about the half-lie without taking money from him as well. I peck him on the cheek.

Outside, there's a fine drizzle coming down – not ideal fireworks weather, but then again not enough to rain off the whole shebang. I pull up the hood of my sweatshirt and start to run. Just as I reach the museum, I pull my tabard on, over my hoodie. Then I walk round the building, trying all the doors, in the hope of finding one that opens. The first two don't yield, but I catch a glimpse of a man in a cleaner's tunic going in through the next, so I run over and try the door.

It opens. Inside, a guard at a desk glances up as I enter, but he just gestures for me to sign in to a large bound book. How old-fashioned and quaint! I sign 'Felicity Lemon', add the time, and pin on my name badge as I stride away.

The cleaners are gathered round some lockers, throwing in their bags and shoes and calling out friendly greetings. They go quiet as I appear.

'Hi, guys!' I say. 'Just looking for my aunt? Janice (I saw this name in the signing-in book, high enough up the list to have left the locker room by now) – is she about?'

'Why are you wearing that?' The speaker is a large woman, with dark hair tucked neatly up into a headscarf with an African print. She gestures to my tabard.

I giggle. 'Oh . . . Auntie Janice said I could pretend I work here. We're doing this thing at school where we tail people from different professions. You know, to get a feel for what it's like to do different jobs.'

The woman in the headscarf nods. 'Your auntie'll have to clear it with Sandra,' she tells me.

'Is Sandra about?'

'She's here somewhere. She's always dashing around, that one!'

'I'll tell Auntie Janice to clear it with her,' I say, and I stride from the room.

I get my bearings quickly, and head straight to the stairs leading down to the old boiler. The hunk of defunct machinery is as I left it – dusty, apart from the area behind it. I rummage in my backpack for my head torch, then I pull up my hood, fit the torch harness over the top, and wriggle through the hole.

I'm in darkness, lit only by the funnel of light

from my torch beam. The unlit areas are shadowy, and this place has got no less creepy since I was last down here. Images of big men with shovels – or, worse, knives – flash through my imagination. Then Poirot appears beside me, friendly and reassuring:

'*Eh bien, Agathe* – I hope you are not forgetting you are the daughter of Clara, *agent extraordinaire?*'

Feeling braver, I plough on through the tunnels, semi-crawling past brick walls, then concrete, until the space opens out at the old Tube station and I can stand up in the tiled corridor.

I stop for a moment, checking for sounds of other human activity. A large grey rat appears in front of me. It isn't scared at all: we eyeball one another. At last, probably realising I am neither food nor proffering food, it ambles away, sniffing at the air as it goes. Meanwhile, I've conjured up a map of this underground area in my mind's eye. The Bank of England is only linked from here by rail – by the Waterloo and City line that doesn't run on Sundays. I'm starting to doubt all my choices. I've wasted precious time blagging my way into the museum just to get down here, and I'm still a distance from the Bank of England. What exactly am I planning on doing when I get there, anyway?

What if Brianna and Liam haven't picked up my text asking them to call the police?

I take out my mobile but there's no signal down here. I will just have to find a way to slow down the robbers when I get there.

I begin to run – slowly to start with, then building up a good rhythm.

I stop after about ten minutes. I'm making quick progress, but my ribs feel like they can't contain my overstretched lungs and racing heart. I clutch my sides and wait for my breathing to settle. There's a scorching in my throat and I'm desperate for a drink.

This is when the first fireworks go off, right above my head. I check my watch in the beam from my head torch: seven o'clock precisely. How did it get so late? At least I must be nearly there, if the display is so close. I begin to jog again, making my way through the last bit of tunnel. And that's when I hear it: a double report of explosions, above and below ground simultaneously – the fireworks and the thermite going off in perfect sync.

The attack on the bank vault has begun.

Ahead, there's a makeshift tunnel leading off from the official one – just like the previous passage I found with Brianna, the one that had caved in. My sense of direction informs me that this tunnel leads directly beneath the Bank of England. Here is where the robbers will have entered. I don't want to tackle them alone, but I don't have anyone with me, and my phone still has no signal.

Then I remember the pager Wallace Jones gave me. I fish it out and, with nervous, fumbling fingers, key in the numbers from the note: 6662.

Another firework goes off – in time with another underground explosion – this one extra loud and ominously close. My hunch was definitely right. They are trying to enter the bank vaults.

Whoever Wallace sends, they will not materialise instantly through a handy portal. I look around for anything else that might help me – and spot a phone, fixed to the wall – clearly designed for emergency use by engineers working on the Tube tracks. I pick up the receiver and am immediately connected to the operator.

'Transport for London emergency services. How can I help you?' says a woman's voice.

'Yes, hello, there's a burglary in progress at the Bank of England. You need to send the police.'

There's a pause – *Argh, there's no time for pauses!* – then she says, 'Is this a prank call?'

'No. You have to listen to me. I'm going to try to slow them down, but there's a group of people attempting to rob the Bank of England as we speak. They're breaking into the underground gold vaults.'

'And you want me to call the police?'

'Yes. Call the police and tell them what I've just told you.' I hang up and sprint through the remaining length of tunnel. Ahead, I can see light where there shouldn't be any. Is there a floodlight down here? Dust motes choke the air like a strange underground fog: presumably rubble dust, from the two explosions. I slow my running to a jog as I get nearer.

I'm squinting from the darkness into the light,

trying to make out details as I move cautiously towards it, when someone grabs me from behind. I'm thrown against the rough wall of the makeshift tunnel with such force that I'm winded and momentarily defenceless.

I rally with a kick to the shin, and my assailant cries out in pain. I step away from the wall and focus on remaining loose – something that Mr Zhang keeps trying (and failing) to teach me. I guess I'm just a naturally tense person. As the man – it is a man, and he is tall and solid as a wall, not my first choice of sparring partner – reaches to grab me, I don't resist; instead, I let him take my arm but I continue moving it in the same direction, so that he is set off balance by the continued arc of my limb through the air. I nearly cheer as, with my next move, I take advantage of him being wrong-footed and send him flailing to the ground. Mr Zhang would be so proud! But where did this man come from? Is he a lookout, placed here by the bank robbers?

I don't wait for my attacker to get up – I'm racing through the newly dug tunnel into the thick fog. I squint and make out ahead the outline of a rope ladder, leading still further below ground. I grab it and descend. My head torch emits a wavering light as I go down, but I can see that the area below me has been lit by battery-powered lamps. I don't know whether I'm racing away from one attacker towards a room full of them, but I have to take the chance. Down and down I climb, and I have an image of Alice falling down the rabbit hole. There must be a bottom to this pit somewhere . . .

12.

LAND OF GOLD

I arrive, at last, at the bottom and jump to the ground. I'm pretty sure the ladder is already twitching with the weight of another human coming down it. I glance up the ladder, but without a large knife – I think with longing of the broadsword that Mr Zhang lets me use for training – I can't think of any way to damage the ladder, to make it harder for my pursuer to get down.

Instead, I glance around. I'm deep underground. The light, though, is almost blinding, and I have to squint to make out where I am. Then I take in the astonishing view: I'm in an enormous room, furnished entirely with blue metal shelving. Each set of shelves has four tiers – and each tier is stacked with gold ingots. The room is basically filled with gold. In contrast with the value of the room's contents, there's only bare wooden flooring and strip lighting. I have a moment's flashback to the sugar maze – but no madman has created this place. I'm deep in the vaults of the Bank of England, and the shimmering piles, bouncing the light around the room, are gold bullion.

'Hey!'

A figure moves towards me, then two more. There's something familiar about them – the way they carry themselves and the authority they give off, like senior civil servants.

I back away – and straight into the welcoming arms of my assailant, who's just made it down the ladder.

'Got you.' He's right: he has me held so tightly I can't move any part of my body. I try to squirm and wriggle, but there's no chance to free myself. I go limp, hoping to take him off-guard, but he just tightens his grip and yanks me back to a standing position. His body is like a brick wall behind me. He lifts me and carries me to one side, away from the rope ladder, my only escape route. Only now does the seriousness of my situation hit me. I'm deep underground, where no one is likely to rescue me. I'm not even sure the Transport for London phone operator I spoke to believed me enough to alert the police. If Liam and Brianna picked up my text, they may already have dialled 999. I hope so. But is there any chance help will arrive soon enough?

My breathing is coming fast and noisy as my thoughts whirl with possible scenarios of what could happen to me: being abandoned deep in the bank vaults where I might never be found – or only discovered when it's too late; being tied up by my captor and dumped on a Tube track; or . . .

Enough! I tell myself. *Mr Zhang didn't train you to lose the plot the minute things got scary.* I close my eyes and slow my breathing, focusing on emptying my mind – which is much trickier than it sounds. Then, with a clearer head, I open my eyes and ask, 'What are you going to do with me?'

'Depends.'

'On what?'

'On whether you cooperate. And on what *he* says.'

I look around, but can only see the team of robbers filling trolleys with stacks of gold ingots. They are methodical, each one knowing his or her role. Once a trolley's full, it's wheeled to the base of the ladder, and hauled up using a rope and pulley system that seems to have appeared, seemingly out of nowhere. The empty trolley is then lowered for refilling.

And then a voice speaks, from among the stacks of gold. 'Really, Byron – it took you two attempts to restrain her? She's a thirteen-year-old girl, for heaven's sake. How on earth did she get away the first time?'

That voice – I know it. I close my eyes and pull up my identification files, running through the categories, knowing I'll get there if I can pin down his appearance:

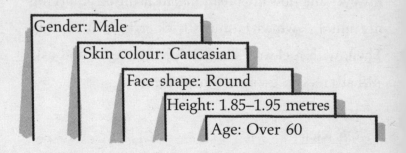

Gender: Male
Skin colour: Caucasian
Face shape: Round
Height: 1.85–1.95 metres
Age: Over 60

I hear heavy, confident footsteps and my eyes flick open. I know who I'm dealing with. But I don't want to believe it.

And then an all-too-familiar figure comes into view.

'Mr Jones!' I exclaim. My mind rebels at the possibility he could be a traitor. I run through everything I've observed about Wallace Jones, and this just can't be really happening.

'Yes, it's me, Agatha. Thank you so much for the "heads-up", as I believe you youngsters call it.'

When I stare blankly at him, he fills in the gap. 'The pager alert you so kindly sent.'

I groan. The pager was why I encountered Byron in the tunnel – the gadget's tracker told Wallace Jones my precise location, and he was able to send his heavy to intercept me. Any remaining hope that Mr Jones is going to save me and foil the plot seeps from me. I feel fury rise up in my chest and throat – at myself, for my carelessness, and at Wallace Jones, for his betrayal.

'This can't be true,' I shout. 'You're a Gatekeeper.

You're supposed to risk your life to protect the country. But you're just . . . a traitor!' Byron tightens his grip on my arms and I yelp in pain.

Wallace Jones smiles a sweet, confiding smile. 'Have you any idea how difficult it is to live on a Gatekeeper's salary, my dear? If the Guild valued us long-servers sufficiently, there would be no need to resort to such tactics. I mean, you didn't think I *chose* to keep working to such a ripe old age, did you? This is my pension.' His eyes harden; I haven't seen his face so . . . mean before. His gaze switches to Byron. 'Right. Tie the girl up and bring her with us – we can't risk her being found down here. She'll give the whole game away.'

I attempt to struggle as Byron loosens his grip just enough to draw a length of rope from his pocket and tie my hands together. Another, longer rope is looped round my legs and drawn tight. For the second time in two days, I find myself thrown over someone's shoulder like a sack of flour. I only realise how sore I am from the last time when the same bruises are bumped again.

We arrive back at the rope ladder, and I can't imagine how Byron will get up the rungs with me over his shoulder. Wallace Jones goes first, and I'm curious to see how he manages. I can't imagine him doing anything so undignified as climbing a rope ladder. But I nearly laugh out loud when he climbs into an empty trolley and is hauled up by his men working the pulley system at the top. We can hear their grunts of effort all the way down the shaft. Surely Wallace Jones can't weigh as much as a trolley-load of gold?

Now for us. Byron unties my feet and hands, and gestures for me to climb the ladder ahead of him. He holds a knife and makes it clear what he'll do with it if I try to get away. He doesn't need to use words to make his intention clear.

I know I should be terrified – and my legs do feel wobbly as I climb the long ladder – but, thanks to that moment's meditation a few minutes earlier, a strange calmness has settled in my mind. It's as if everything has led up to this moment. I'm thankful for the martial arts lessons with Mr Zhang, which have got me to peak fitness, because I arrive at the top barely out of breath.

I'm also, however, only just ahead of Byron. I step to one side and gauge my chances of escape. If he's only got the knife, it might be worth running – but what if he has a gun? Mr Zhang hasn't taught me any moves for dodging bullets.

I decide it's not worth the risk. Byron reaches me and swiftly reties my limbs and throws me back over his shoulder. As he strides through the newly blasted tunnel, I crane my neck, trying to spot anything that might help me get away. But there is only dust and rubble.

After a bumpy walk across stones and concrete, we arrive at Bank station. There's a Waterloo and City line train waiting, carriage doors open and engine rumbling. We have to wait on the platform while the trolley-loads of bullion are spread across several carriages. Byron sets me on my feet, but my wrists and ankles are still tied, so I'm like a convict in shackles. The ropes are cutting into my skin, and I want to ask Byron to loosen them, but I'm not sure what his temper is like, and I'm nervous of angering a man of his stature.

To distract myself, I take the opportunity to count the conspirators: twelve men and women, plus Byron and Jones. None of them have bothered to cover their faces, which worries me. They weren't expecting any witnesses – now they have one. What will they do with me, the only witness, after this? If I do survive, I'll need to be able to identify them, so I decide to take advantage of their lack of disguise to study them.

– I observe each person in turn, and store their details in my identification files. There are two men who look so alike they must be twins: both short, with dark hair and blue eyes. There's an old, white-haired man, so bent and wizened that I'm astonished he's part of the gang. But he heaves the stacks of gold ingots like a much younger man, hardly pausing for breath. There's a thin, pale woman with waist-length red hair – like in the Pre-Raphaelite paintings my mum took me to see when I was little. The remaining eight members of the crew are less distinguishable. I make a mental note of any features that might help – glasses, freckles, a beauty spot or a bald patch – but they all look just like ordinary people you might see in the street. What has brought them together? I notice again the way they hold themselves, as if they're important in some way. Could they also be Gatekeepers?

Despite the gravity of their task, there's an atmosphere of excitement. They swear and shout instructions, but, in between, they laugh and joke, clearly relieved at the success of their heist.

At last, all the gold has been loaded on to the train, and the twelve crew members have taken their seats on board. Byron picks me up, and he and Wallace Jones step into the first carriage, among the stacks of bullion. I'm dumped unceremoniously on to a double seat, and my head bangs against the side of the carriage.

'Careful, Byron – she might as well enjoy the ride. It's going to be her last,' says Jones. His voice holds no trace of either sympathy or compassion, nor any of the gentleness he'd shown when I first met him.

Sociopath, I decide. The bad thing about sociopaths

is that in extreme cases they don't value the life of anyone but themselves, and I've already decided that Wallace Jones is an extreme case. The good thing about sociopaths is that they tend to be quite vain. Maybe I can use this to my advantage.

Jones sits opposite me and peers out of the window as the train pulls out of the station.

'So, this is a very complex plot,' I say.

He looks very pleased with himself. 'Yes; it was all my own idea. Clever, isn't it?'

'Very. So . . . who are the others?'

He raises an eyebrow. 'My team? Oh . . . others who've been let down.'

'By the Gatekeepers' Guild?' I ask him. 'How on earth did you manage to convince them all to go along with your plan?'

He beams and leans eagerly towards me. 'I am quite good at persuading people to do things. I have the gift of the gab, I suppose.'

I push on with my questioning. 'Tell me – how did you get the date of the fireworks moved from November to cover the heist? And to a Sunday too?'

'Ahh.' He taps the side of his nose. 'Friends in high places, don't you know.'

'What . . . like . . . *the Lord Mayor?*'

He shakes his head, smiling, as if he's indulging a naughty child. 'You know I can't tell you that.'

I decide to change tack, to appeal to his love of talking. Anything to establish any kind of bond, to delay him from having me killed.

'Can you tell me about my mum?'

He turns surprised eyes on me. 'Clara? What do you want to know?'

I shrug. 'How well did you know her?'

'She was one of a kind, your mother. Surprisingly tough for such a delicate-looking creature – and so quick-witted!'

'How do you mean?'

'She could solve any puzzle, any code, put before her. She was faster than our most experienced codebreakers. They hated her!' He laughs. 'They had a name for her, er, what was it . . .?'

He goes into a reverie, and I have to prompt him: 'The nickname?'

'Oh, yes. It was "Wise Cracker" – you know, a pun on how she cracked codes, but also how she thought she knew everything.'

'Did you think she was like that?'

He looks surprised again. 'Not at all. She was the most modest woman I've known. If anything, she underestimated her gifts. In fact, I blame her modesty for her demise . . .' He catches my eye and tails off abruptly.

I feel as if someone's clutched my heart in a cold fist. 'You know how she died? Tell me!'

He glances at Byron, who's standing in the aisle, like an ominous shadow looming over me. 'Are you sure she's tied up correctly? The ropes look a bit loose.'

Byron leans over and tugs on my bindings. I grit my teeth as I feel them dig still further into my flesh.

'They're sound,' he says. 'I know my knots.'

'I'm sure you do; I'm sure you do,' says Jones, absent-mindedly. 'We must be nearly there by now.'

I don't want us to be 'nearly there'. I don't want to arrive at the next leg of our journey, and discover what their plans are for me. I don't want to be disposed of, or abandoned in a dark pit from which there's no escape. And I don't want to miss an opportunity to find out what really happened to Mum.

'Tell me!' I cry out. 'What happened to my mother?'

It's my last chance. The train begins to slow and my heart, in contrast, begins to race. Normally, I would have loved a train ride on a privately chartered train. I would have enjoyed the movement and the blur through the window, and I would have felt privileged. Today, though, the train's emptiness only reminds me how isolated I am. I give way to this feeling again for a moment, remembering anew that nobody knows where I am.

My mobile . . .! Is there any chance I can get a signal? And how can I reach my phone, with my hands tied? I glance at my feet and realise with a pang my backpack's been left behind. So that's it then. I can only hope Wallace Jones doesn't really care about killing me – if I'm lucky, he'll opt instead for just keeping me tied up, until he and the others have got away.

I recommence my questions. 'I haven't asked you *why* you had to move the fireworks from November to September,' I say. 'Couldn't you have waited and carried out the robbery when the fireworks are normally held?'

His watery eyes wander back to focus on me. 'Oh, the financial savings laws are changing,' he says vaguely. 'I need to get the gold offshore before the new regulations came in.'

'So . . . you're breaking the law, to make sure you don't break the law?'

Wallace Jones turns an alarming shade of red, and I instantly regret provoking him. At Mr Zhang's I haven't got to the bit about defending myself when my hands and legs are tied. If I survive this experience, I'll definitely request it. Along with any bullet-dodging moves. Maybe he can give me some superhero powers while he's at it too.

Jones's spittle hits my face as he protests angrily. 'I wouldn't have to break the law if those in power at the Gatekeepers' Guild weren't so keen to keep the rest of us in poverty.'

I glance at his clothing. It's impossible to attend a school full of rich students and not learn how to spot expensive clothes. He's wearing at least a thousand pounds' worth of suit – and I reckon his shoes cost a good five hundred. This is not a man who is living below the poverty line. I think of Dad, with his ancient, ugly, scratchy suit, and how he never complains about having so little money to spend on himself. I can't stop a tear from running down my face, as I realise that, if I go missing, Dad might soon have more money to spend on himself. He also might never find out what happened to his only child.

We arrive at the British Museum station, where the gold is loaded into crates on the back of a truck, and driven towards the secret dock. I watch the stacks of ingots leave the train, and with each one I feel my chances of survival dwindle. Wallace Jones steps down and Byron slings me back over his shoulder and jogs off the train and towards the dock, passing Jones on the way.

'All right, Byron, let's not show off, shall we?' calls

Jones, mildly. 'You may have the brawn, but I definitely have the brain.'

Byron just grunts in response, and I get the impression he isn't that keen on his boss. If I had more time, I might be able to turn him – but we're about to enter the dock, so time's running out fast.

'Mr Byron,' I try. He grunts, which I decide to take as encouragement. 'He doesn't treat you with much respect, does he? Mr Jones, I mean.' Another grunt. 'Why don't you take over? The gold's already been stolen; the plan's all gone well . . .' No answer. 'I mean, Mr Jones might have been useful for his contacts, but do you really still need him?'

'And do you ever shut up?' he says eventually.

'Not very often,' I admit.

'Well, try it now, and I might let you live a little longer.'

I decide to take his advice.

13.

A COLD DIP

At the dock, with the entry doors closed behind us and two Gatekeepers posted as guards, Byron unties me again. I rub my sore wrists where the rope has dug in.

'Just don't try anything,' he says.

We stand as a group beside the truck filled with gold and wait. Jones is having some kind of discussion on a walkie-talkie. After a couple of minutes, the water in front of us surges upwards and a white submarine emerges. Despite my dire circumstances, I can't help feeling a thrill of excitement at seeing it rise from the water. How many people can say they've watched a submarine come to the surface? It looks a lot like a small private plane, except that it hasn't got any wings. It has a tall piece on top near the back, that sticks up like a fin. Not quite *Thunderbird 4*, but still pretty exciting.

'What do you think of our transport, Miss Oddlow?' says Jones. He looks, if possible, even prouder of himself than he did earlier.

I hesitate. Flattery hasn't got me released, so I decide to try confrontation. 'It's a bit rusty,' I say, pointing to a brown patch on the submarine's side. 'Are you sure it's watertight?'

He frowns at me. 'Why is she untied?' he asks Byron.

Byron shrugs. 'Didn't seem much point keeping her tied up in here – there's nowhere for her to go.'

'Well, tie her back up, will you?'

Byron shrugs again and starts to pull a rope from his pocket. I'm keeping one eye on him as I watch the truck advance towards the submarine. Its driver is the red-haired woman; her hair is like a beacon down here, where everything else is grey or black.

The claws of a crane on the back of the truck seize the first crate and start hoisting it upwards.

I have an idea which might slow things down, at least. As Byron takes a step towards me, I sprint round him, reaching the crane just as it starts to swing into position ready to lower the crate of gold. A man has climbed out of the submarine and has his arms outstretched, waiting to receive the delivery. In one smooth move, amid the startled cries from those around me, I jump up to where the truck driver sits, reach in front of her, and pull the lever that will release the gold. The crate tumbles from the crane's claws, hits the top of the submarine and lurches off into the water, drenching everyone standing close by.

Wallace Jones is one of the bystanders who gets soaked. He lets out a roar of anger at seeing his gold hit the water. His hair is dripping, and he pushes it impatiently back from his face.

'Can you reach any of it?' he yells, looking down from the side of the dock and waving his arms around in distress. He reminds me of a spoilt little boy watching his favourite toy boat take in water and sink in a pond.

The man on the submarine vanishes back down inside and reappears with a diver's suit. He steps into the suit and pulls it on. Within seconds, he's fitted his breathing apparatus and has dived into the water to hunt for the fallen gold.

Wallace Jones turns to me with the same red-faced fury I caught a glimpse of on the underground train. I know I'm in trouble now – but I've created the distraction I wanted. He advances towards me and I'm suddenly aware of how big he is. When I met him at the Gatekeepers' Guild headquarters, he was like a large, welcoming uncle. Now he is a looming threat.

I'm amazed when Byron steps between us.

'Leave her,' he says quietly.

'This is your fault, Byron. If you'd tied her up, as I asked, she wouldn't have managed to release that crate into the water. You'll pay for this out of your cut.'

'I don't like your tone.' says his henchman, calmly.

'Don't forget this was entirely my plan. You are worth nothing without me,' sneers Jones.

The crane is moving again, and I get ready for another sabotage attack. But Jones spots me.

'You don't really think you can pull off the same trick twice, do you? Haven't you heard the expression, "Fool me once, shame on you; fool me twice, shame on me"?'

'How about, "Rob the Bank of England, shame on you"? Have you heard that one?' I ask him.

He goes – if possible – even redder. His colour is actually deepening to something close to purple. I wonder if he might be about to pass out. At least that would buy me more time to escape.

No such luck. Instead, Wallace Jones walks towards me and picks me up by the hood of my sweatshirt. I barely have time to process the realisation that he is far stronger than I'd imagined, as I'm suddenly suspended over the dark water. He holds me at arm's length, so I can't use any moves to defend myself.

'Not so talkative now, are we, Agatha Oddlow? Your mother wasn't half as annoying.'

I play for time. 'So do you know how she died?'

He laughs. 'Is that really what you want to talk about right now? I'd focus on your own life, if I were you. Doesn't look like it's going to last much longer.'

I stare down into the water. I can't see anything below the dark surface. How cold will it be? Too cold for the human body to survive the shock, no doubt.

'Please don't,' I say.

'"*Please don't,*"' he mimics, in a high-pitched voice. 'You regret your actions now, eh?'

'I don't regret anything,' I say fiercely – and rather recklessly.

'Well, that makes two of us,' he says.

And then he drops me.

14.

A SWEATSHIRT IN THE WORKS

The water feels freezing, even after the coolness of the cave. I know it's important to float for a moment until I catch my breath, to avoid cold-water shock, but first I have to get out of sight of the people on land. I need them to believe I've drowned, so they don't come looking for me. I manage to swim round to the far side of the submarine, where I can't be seen. I lie on my back and open my arms and legs, like a starfish. From here, I can see the back of the man who's receiving the gold from the crane. It looks like he has other people inside the sub, helping him to receive the gold.

My teeth are chattering, but I know I have a greater chance of surviving here in the cold (but thankfully not *too* cold) water than I do on land in the company of Wallace Jones. I don't think Byron would have killed me, whatever Jones's instructions, but now I don't have to put that hunch to the test.

I can hear Jones's booming voice, even from here: 'Is she dead? Can anyone see her?'

Byron answers, but I can't make out what he's saying.

'Come on, everyone!' shouts Jones. 'That's the brat done with – just get on with your jobs, for heaven's sake! What are you waiting for? The police to arrive?'

I've done it – they think I'm dead. My breathing slows, both with relief and with my body adapting to the water temperature. Now I need to act fast. I only have until all the gold is on board to stop the robbers from leaving.

I take a deep breath and dive beneath the submarine. It's pitch black, and I have to feel my way round the underside of its hull. What can I do down here, to delay them, with no weapons? I swim back to the surface and close my eyes so I can Change Channel. I summon up a mental photograph of a diagram I once saw of a submarine. There are valves to let air in and out, to help the machine to descend and ascend, plus a rudder, and a propeller—

The propellers – that's it! I have a sudden flashback of Alesky, the taxi driver on Sloane Street, removing the plastic bin liner from the wheel of his cab. I need to jam the propeller, which should be at the back of the vessel. But I'm treading water, without a single tool to hand. What on earth can I use?

I realise my clothes are the only thing I have. It takes my weary arms a ridiculous length of time to remove my sweatshirt, which is stuck to my body as if it has suction cups. At last, I succeed. But I can hear the engine of the sub starting up – time is running out.

With one last push, I dive to the back of the submarine. The propeller is already turning, and I'm terrified of getting my hand or even my whole arm mangled in the blades. But the sub may be leaving at any moment – and I can't let Wallace Jones get away.

Gingerly, I begin to poke one sleeve of my sweatshirt towards the propeller; it snags, and there's a guttural sound, as if the propeller is choking. Then the entire garment is yanked from my grasp as it gets wound round the blades, and I have to let go quickly, to avoid being dragged into the spinning trap myself.

I smile briefly at the success of my plan. With one last push, I make it back to the surface. I'm so cold and tired I can't feel my limbs. My body is a weightless empty vessel and I'm floating. There are lights bobbing about prettily around the dock – fireflies? Nothing makes sense any more. And then everything goes dark.

15.

RESCUED!

It feels like I have an eel down my throat that is being hauled out. I'm gagging, choking, vomiting . . . And all the while, someone is stroking my back and saying, 'That's right – get it all out.'

At last, the gagging stops. I lie on my side, gasping. My throat is stinging, and everything aches. And I'm cold – so very, very cold. My teeth won't stop chattering and my whole body is clenching, locking up with cold.

Someone shouts, 'Can we have some blankets over here?' A moment later, I'm being wrapped up like a child after a hot bath, and carried – oh, the bliss of being carried . . .

I close my eyes and fall asleep.

Bright lights – too bright. And white everywhere – white walls, white furniture . . . And that smell – illness and disinfectant . . . *Hospital.* I feel a strong sense of déjà vu.

'She's awake!' Liam's voice is calling to someone, who looms into view.

'Dad!' My voice is croaky and my throat's raw.

Dad sits on a chair beside my bed and takes my hand. 'You've got to stop scaring me like this.'

'Sorry.'

'You should be. Dashing after crooks and villains without any thought for your poor old dad.'

'I did think of you,' I croak. 'I thought about how you'd never know what happened to me if I died.' I smile.

'Do you have any idea how long we've been waiting for you to wake up?' asks Liam.

I frown. Have I been asleep for more than a couple of hours?

'Eighteen hours,' he says.

The shock must show in my face, because he laughs. 'Yep – a lot's been happening while you were sleeping like a fairy-tale princess.' I pull a face at him, and he laughs again.

'So,' he continues, 'do you want to know what happened, after you conked out?' He walks closer, so I can see him.

Dad holds up a hand. 'She's just woken up, Liam. Let's get Agatha checked over before you start overwhelming her with information.'

'I'll fetch a nurse,' says Liam. While he's gone, Dad holds my hand and smiles down at me. I close my eyes for a moment or two. I feel so safe and warm that I nearly drift off to sleep again, but a nurse's voice snaps me back to the present.

'I hear our patient's awake. Let's have a look at you.' She picks up my wrist to check my pulse but first she peers into my face with a kind expression. 'I've been wondering what colour eyes you have. Lovely deep blue, aren't they?'

I smile. *Shade 2B on my eye-colour chart.*

She takes my blood pressure and nods in approval. 'You've come out of this pretty well, young lady. No more dips in underground waterways for you, though.'

I laugh, but it hurts my throat and I wince.

'Yes – I understand you vomited up quite a lot of water. You'll be sore for a while,' she tells me. She makes some notes on a handheld electronic device, then turns to Dad. 'I'll leave you to it,' she says, and walks out, shutting the door behind her.

Liam comes straight back in and Dad gestures for him to perch on the edge of my bed, which he does.

'So you don't even know how it ended,' he bursts out. 'They caught them all! Even that traitor Jones – and all thirteen of his co-conspirators.'

Relief fills my lungs. I hadn't realised how tense I'd been, waiting to have this confirmed.

'It was so lucky that the submarine broke down like that,' says Liam.

I shake my head. 'Sweatshirt,' I tell him.

'Sweatshirt?' He frowns in bemusement.

'In the propeller.'

His eyes grow wide. 'That was such a clever idea! I'd never have thought of that!'

I feel a blush rise to my cheeks.

'Don't encourage her,' says Dad. 'It was foolhardy and reckless.'

'True,' says Liam. 'Really clever, though.' He looks me over, assessing my fragile state. 'Are you up to hearing the rest of the story?'

I hesitate. The little bit of energy I had when I woke up has already drained away, and I feel exhausted. My arms and legs are like lead and it feels as if my brain's full of cotton wool – all fuzz and no substance. I nearly tell him I have to sleep. I have an image of that dark, deep water – of what it felt like to be suspended above it by Wallace Jones, knowing he didn't care what happened to me. I shiver.

'Are you cold, love?' asks Dad, tucking the hospital blanket more closely round me.

I shake my head. 'No . . .' I fix my eyes on Liam. 'Tell me what happened,' I say hoarsely.

'OK . . .' He hitches himself up a bit more on the end of my bed. 'So after you messaged me and Brianna, we tried to get back in touch with you, but we couldn't reach you, so we called the professor. Luckily, she guessed you'd be at the underground dock. That place is amazing!' He looks a bit shamefaced. 'Me and Brianna weren't actually meant to go there – but we couldn't stay away knowing you might be in danger. We got through by going down to the Waterloo and City line at Bank station and then finding the newly dug tunnels. We did have to wait for the Guild to turn up, so we could get into the dock. They were all a bit distracted, so we just followed them and they didn't seem to notice.

'The Guild . . .?' says Dad.

'Oh . . . I mean the professor,' says Liam quickly.

Dad frowns. 'So that officer from the Metropolitan Police who came round to the cottage to thank you, after the whole incident with the water pollution . . .?'

'She's in a guild of senior police detectives,' says

Liam quickly. I'm pleased with this response, which Dad seems to accept. 'So, anyway,' Liam continues, 'they found you and dragged you out – it was Brianna who spotted you with these amazing torches she'd brought with her.'

'The fireflies,' I tell them.

'Right . . .' says Liam, nodding like he's humouring a dangerous lunatic. 'Anyway, while you were being dragged out, that Wallace Jones guy and the rest of the gang were being encircled and arrested. Only one of them – a huge bloke, bodyguard-type – tried to resist.'

Byron, I decide. 'Did he get away?'

'The big guy?' he asks. I nod. 'No. He was caught by two officers and well and truly restrained.'

'That's good,' I say.

Liam's eyes are sparkling – he clearly feels he's had a great adventure.

'Sorry you missed the fireworks,' I croak, and Liam laughs.

'Oh, don't worry – this was way more exciting.' He catches Dad's eye and turns pale. 'I don't mean . . .

I don't . . . I just . . . Well, I'm glad you're OK, obviously.'

'Obviously,' murmurs Dad sarcastically.

'Er . . . well . . . I'll leave you to it,' says Liam.

I wave goodbye and sit in silence with my dad, relishing the feeling of being clean, dry and safe, with his big, warm hand holding mine.

After a few minutes, he clears his throat. 'Listen, love, about Cornwall . . .'

I take a deep breath and force myself to say, 'You did really well to get that job. You deserve it – you work so hard.'

He squeezes my hand. 'Thank you for that – I know how much it cost you. Anyway, I turned it down.'

I stare at him.

'It was going to be such an upheaval,' he continues. 'I like it here – don't you?'

I nod. My eyes well up with relief, but he pretends not to notice.

'Good,' he says, nodding. 'Well, that works out for both of us then.'

'Dad . . .?'

'Yes, love?'

'Will you regret it?' The words come out as a rasp from my sore, raw throat.

'What? Not taking the job? I did think long and hard about it. There'll be other opportunities, but now is not the right time for us to be moving and having to start all over again somewhere else. We both have too many friends here. And I love the park. And Groundskeeper's Cottage.'

'Me too,' I croak. The stone in my belly is shrinking. It's a pebble – no, a tiny piece of gravel – no, a grain of sand, a speck of dust . . . Now it's dwindled to nothing. I find myself beaming at him.

16.

EPILOGUE

I've had all week off school to recover from my near-drowning incident. I open the front door on Saturday morning to find an old friend on the doorstep.

'Surprise!'

I haven't seen JP since he stopped living in the park. He's been way too busy with his new job.

'JP!' I give him a big hug, then take a step back to admire his new look – he no longer looks like a rough sleeper, but is dressed smart-casual, in a V-neck navy sweater over a light-blue shirt, with navy chinos. 'You look good.'

'Thank you,' he says. 'I'm earning money again – it's been a revelation.'

'Come in!' I say, stepping back to let him into the house.

'JP – great to see you.' Dad has been waiting in the hallway to greet him, and they shake hands.

'You too, Rufus.'

They stand about, smiling stupidly at each other, until I say, 'Oh, for heaven's sake, you're grown men – you can give each other a hug without being so childish about it.'

They laugh and do as I suggest.

We're still standing in the hall when there's another knock at the door. I glance at Dad. 'What's going on?'

'Just open it,' he says, with a smile.

This time, Professor Dorothy D'Oliveira is on the doorstep, neatly dressed in a lightweight pink coat and matching hat and shoes.

'Hello, Agatha. May I come in?' she asks.

'Sure . . .' I say. She isn't frowning, so she can't be about to find some new way of firing me.

She, Dad and Rufus greet one another politely, then Dad takes their coats, hangs these on the coat hooks on the wall, and shows our guests through to the living room. It's all surprisingly formal. I'm just going in to join them when there's a third knock at the door.

'Can you get that, Aggie?' says Dad.

'OK . . .' This is getting distinctly weird. This time, Liam and Brianna are on the doorstep.

'I brought a cake,' says Liam, holding up a white cardboard box. It has no logo on it, so I can't tell which shop it's from. I let them in and, while they're slinging their coats over the bannisters, I ask, 'What are we celebrating?'

'Your birthday, dummy!' says Brianna, with a laugh. She takes in my gobsmacked expression. 'You didn't forget your own birthday, did you?'

'I guess I just lost track of the date.' I do some calculations. 'Hold on – it's on Monday. Isn't today Saturday?'

'We thought we'd do it today – much more fun than on your first day back at school,' says Liam.

Brianna is shaking her head at me in wonder. 'Agatha Oddlow, you're the only girl I know who can forget her own birthday.'

I pull a face. 'Hey! I'm older than you, you know.'

She rolls her eyes. 'Yeah, by a whole five weeks.'

'Five *and a half*,' I correct her. 'Let's see this cake then.'

'All in good time,' says Liam, mysteriously. 'Is anyone else here?'

'JP and Professor D'Oliveira.'

They seem to be expecting this. I lead them through to the living room, where we file in and take seats between the adults, who are talking about Wallace Jones.

'So he really isn't going to get charged?' Dad is asking.

The professor shakes her head. 'It certainly looks that way. Do you know what really gets my goat?'

'What's that?' asks Dad.

'I trusted that man.'

'Oh, so you knew him?'

She nods. 'Only through my work on the police force. He was part of national security, so we had to work together from time to time, running protection for high-profile events.' She shakes her head. 'Because of him, I've found myself questioning my own instincts. I thought I was a better judge of character.'

'But he believed he was right about everything,' I point out.

'How do you mean?'

I've spent all week thinking about this. I was as shaken as the professor to find I'd liked and trusted a traitor. 'He didn't give off evil vibes, because he didn't think he was doing anything wrong. He had basically convinced himself that he deserved everything he tried to steal.' I get into my stride. 'I mean, normally people are aware when they're doing something wrong – but someone like Jones, who saw everything only from his own point of view, believed he was always right. You'd never guess he was anything other than genuine, because he'd never seem unsure or guilty – he'd never do anything to make you suspicious of him.'

The professor considers this. 'Something like a narcissistic personality disorder? You may be right there. But I will still be more cautious from now on – the fact someone like that could fool everyone . . .' She sighs. 'But we are not here to waste our breath on such a man.'

'No – we're here to celebrate Agatha!' shouts Liam, making everyone jump. 'Sorry – got a big carried away there,' he says, with a blush. 'Where should I put this?' He holds up the cake box, which he's been cradling on his lap, and Dad escorts him and the cake through to the kitchen.

The rest of us sit in silence, until JP says, 'Oh – I brought you this!' He produces a small package from his pocket. It's wrapped in gold and tied with a purple ribbon and is a beautiful thing in its own right. He hands it to me.

'Ooh, a present!' I clap my hands like a toddler. I can't help it – I love getting gifts. 'Shall I wait for the others or . . .?'

'Open it now,' says JP, clearly almost as eager as I am.

I untie the ribbon and ease my finger under the sticky tape on the wrapping paper, careful not to tear it. Inside, there is a small box. I lift the lid and gasp at its contents: a silver locket, in the shape of a book, engraved with my initials. 'It's lovely,' I say.

'Open it,' he tells me.

I ease open the hinged door of the locket, and inside find a photo of my mum. It's a miniature version of the photo I keep by my bed, the one of her and her bike. I look at him. 'This is my favourite photo of Mum! Where did you get it?'

'Your dad gave me a copy.'

'It's beautiful – I love it. Thank you so much.' I jump up and give him a kiss on the cheek.

'Me next,' says Brianna, but just then Liam sticks his head round the door, sees what we're doing, and disappears again.

'They are!' we hear him shout. 'They're opening the presents.'

'Well, tell them not to!' comes Dad's voice. 'I want to be there.'

Liam pushes the door open again.

'It's OK, we heard,' I tell him. 'I only opened one, in any case.'

He vanishes again, and a moment later a hand comes round the door to turn off the living-room light. Then Dad and Liam enter the room; Liam is carrying the cake, which is twinkling with candles. Everyone sings 'Happy Birthday', and I blow out my candles. When the lights come back on, I take in the wonder of the cake. Like my new locket, it's in the shape of a book. I read the title on the cover and, underneath it, the name of the author.

Murder at the Museum
Felicity Lemon

'Do you like it?' Liam whispers in my ear. (How did he get there? I didn't see him come over.)

'I love it,' I tell him.

We eat the cake – a delicious Victoria sponge, stuffed with jam and cream – and then I open my remaining presents.

Dad has bought me a knee-length wool coat, with a full skirt and a wide belt. It's almost exactly the same shade of red as my favourite beret.

'But . . . how did you . . .?'

'I had a little help,' he tells me, smiling at Brianna. I mouth my thanks across the room.

'And this is from me,' Brianna says, handing me a plastic bag. 'Sorry – I didn't get time to wrap it.'

It's a chemistry set, complete with a mini Bunsen burner. I hate chemistry lessons, as she knows – but she also knows that doing my own experiments is an entirely different experience from following the teacher's instructions.

'Fantastic – thanks!' I say.

Dad groans. 'Really? Are you trying to encourage her to burn down the house, Brianna?'

She laughs. 'Don't worry, I'll make sure she uses it safely.'

'Hmm,' says Dad doubtfully.

'This is from me,' says the professor, drawing a slim, rectangular parcel from her handbag and handing it to me. I tear off the paper. Inside is a DVD of the film *Alice in Wonderland*. I already own this, but I don't want to be rude.

'Thank you,' I say.

'You're very welcome,' she replies. Then she lowers her voice, 'Watch it when you're alone.'

I look at her in surprise, but she is busy unfolding her serviette and dabbing at the corners of her mouth.

We all have a second slice of cake and more tea (except for me, because I'm on my favourite – hot chocolate), and then we wander out into Hyde Park to enjoy the mid-September sunshine. The leaves are already turning and the colours are beautiful.

This time, it's the professor who appears by my side without warning.

'Before the others come back over, tell me everything you know about the case,' she says quietly.

I fill her in: how the museum attendant was murdered because he must have uncovered the tunnel, and how the clay cup was only stolen to make his murder look like a bungled burglary.

'Did Wallace Jones let slip anything incriminating?' she asks, under cover of admiring some autumn crocuses.

'Not really.' I take a moment to consider what he'd said, and add, 'I asked him how he'd managed to get the date of the fireworks moved, and he said he had "friends in high places", but he wouldn't say who.'

'"Friends in high places"?' She is quiet for a moment. 'I wonder . . . There is someone in local government, whom certain agents believe to be corruptible . . . for a price.'

'So if they were able to move the date of the fireworks somehow . . .'

'. . . then I'm sure our friend Mr Jones would have paid them quite handsomely.'

'Is there any way to check?'

She nods. 'We have someone who can look into it.'

'And is there anything the Guild can do to make sure Wallace Jones goes to prison?'

She shakes her head. 'It's looking doubtful. These "friends in high places" seem to be everywhere.'

I remember all the other Guild agents involved in the robbery. 'I've been wanting to ask you: how did Wallace Jones persuade so many Guild agents to desert?'

'Oh – those weren't Guild agents!' She looks horrified.

I'm confused. 'But Wallace Jones said . . .'

She shakes her head. 'Let me rephrase that. They were not *current* Guild agents. Disgraced, every one of them.'

'So they'd all been fired?'

'Indeed they had. For quite serious misdemeanours, in some cases.'

That makes me feel a lot better. 'And Sofia Solokov?'

'What about her?'

I feel uncomfortable. 'Was she . . .?'

'If you are asking me whether Sofia was involved with this corrupt band of individuals, child, then you can stop right there. I even had her warn you off – don't you remember, when you were investigating the sinkhole?'

'That was her? The woman with the scarf and sunglasses?'

She nods. 'That's right.'

I frown, trying to piece the jigsaw together. 'So you knew . . .?'

She shakes her head. 'All we knew was that someone had caused a cave-in by tampering with the tunnel network. But my agents were already investigating, and it certainly wasn't safe to allow a teenage girl to run around in that area. What's more, we had yet to find out who had caused the damage – a simple saboteur-cum-vandal, or someone with a more organised agenda.'

Liam shouts over: 'Agatha – we're heading over to the fountain. You coming?'

'In a minute!'

The professor takes my hand and places something in the palm – it's cold and heavy. I open my fingers just enough to assure myself it's the key.

'Welcome back, Miss Oddlow,' she says, smiling. 'Now, please try to stick to the rules.'

'I will – I promise. Thank you so much.'

She draws a thick envelope from her handbag.

'I have placed some things you might like in here,' she says, handing me the envelope. 'I had a good old rummage at home, seeing as how the Guild file rooms were no use. These are all from my private records.

Put it away now.' I haven't brought my backpack with me, so I run back to the house and up to the attic, to deposit the package somewhere safe.

When I reach my room, I rethread the key through its silver chain and fasten it round my neck. It feels good to have it back. I tip the contents of the envelope out on to my bed. There's a small bundle of photos and newspaper cuttings about Mum, fastened with a bright-red paperclip. I remove the clip and quickly scan through them. I don't think there's anything groundbreaking here – just stories about Mum and her work keeping the City of London safer. Nothing mentions the Gatekeepers' Guild, of course – it's all presented as though she works for the council or something.

I put the contents back in the envelope and place it carefully on my bedside table, beside Mum's photo, and whisper: 'I will find out who killed you, Mum, I promise.'

Then I race downstairs and out to join my extended family in my favourite London park. They are all standing round the fountain, admiring the water's sparkle – except for Brianna, who is trailing her hand in the water and exclaiming over the chilly temperature.

'You could just not put your hand in it,' Liam points out.

At this, she splashes him and he squeals.

'See – cold, isn't it?'

I walk over to join them. Liam grins at me and rolls his eyes at Brianna's behaviour.

'Come on,' he says, gesturing to a bench nearby. We sit down and watch Brianna, who has taken off her shoes and socks, rolled up her jeans and is now paddling in the fountain. Dad has either not noticed this serious breach of park rules, or is turning a blind eye.

'Are you OK?' Liam asks me.

I meet his eye. 'I wish I knew if I'll ever find out what happened to Mum.'

He reaches out to hold my hand, and I let him. His palm feels warm and smooth.

'You'll find out, Agatha Oddlow. If anyone can solve a mystery, it's you.'

Brianna comes running over and we quickly let

go of each other's hands. She's soaked, and she shakes herself like a dog, spraying us with cold water. Liam and I shriek and make a run for it, with Brianna chasing after us. As I glance back, I can see Dad, JP and Professor D'Oliveira watching on in amusement.

It feels good to be silly and childish for once.

As I run, giggling like a little kid, a familiar figure steps out in front of me and touches his hat in greeting.

'Enjoy your birthday celebration, mam'selle,' says Poirot. 'I am sure we will meet again very soon.'

I nod and smile to him, and carry on running, out of breath and laughing.

ONOMATOPOEIC CIPHER

A – whizz	N – oink
B – achoo	O – jangle
C – sizzle	P – kerplunk
D – beep	Q – meow
E – plop	R – moo
F – brring	S – honk
G – quack	T – belch
H – thwack	U – buzz
I – choo-choo	V – ribbit
J – ding	W – bang
K – glug	X – cheep
L – vroom	Y – guffaw
M – hiccup	Z – argh

ACKNOWLEDGEMENTS

Tibor Jones Studio is about enabling aspiring unpublished writers so that they can work together and bring one voice to these pages for our readers. Via the intrepid spirit of Agatha Oddlow and her guiding star, Agatha Christie, we've been able to interrogate the writing process and ask questions about narrative, creativity and what a good detective story is all about. Joe Heap helped again and Rosie Sandler was instrumental in seeing this through. Charlotte Colwill and Tilda Johnson were fantastic in their creativity and support as were John Bond and Annabelle Wright at Whitefox. A special mention goes to Mrs Graham at Corpus Christi Primary School in Brixton, London, who shared the first book in this series, *Agatha Oddly – The Secret Key*, with her students and won us valuable feedback and, we're delighted to say, rave reviews. She's an incredible teacher who makes reading both fun and liberating. The world needs more Mrs Grahams. We have to thank the team at Tibor Jones, especially Ana Boado, Mary Rodgers and the steadfast Landa Acevedo-Scott, who shared Kevin Conroy Scott's vision of creating stories for children in new and ethical ways. Thanks also to Michelle Misra who is part of a sharp and talented team at HarperCollins in the UK which includes Rachel Denwood, who first saw Agatha lurking round the corner in her beret, ready for her stage, and Carla Alonzi who keeps spreading the word about Agatha around the world. Agatha always dares to be different in her own analogue way and we hope that children can draw inspiration from her quirky pursuit of the truth.